UNFINISHED BUSINESS

Frank and Joe crouched down in the middle of a thick grove of trees, watching Professor Ortega. He was waiting in the clearing at the base of the pyramid for his contact to appear.

"Professor!" The sudden cry came from the top of the pyramid. The Hardys peered up at the man who now stood on the steps of the ancient structure. He was the one who had shot the professor at the airport!

"Professor!" Frank yelled. "Get out of there! It's a trap!"

The assassin clambered down the last few steps of the pyramid toward the professor. Ortega, frightened by the man's sudden advance, stepped back and stumbled, falling to the ground.

Frank saw that this time the man wasn't carrying a gun. He had a machete. The blade glinted in the light as he raised it over his head. "Now, Professor, I'll finish the job."

Books in THE HARDY BOYS CASEFILES® Series

#1	DEAD ON TARGET	#29	THICK AS THIEVES
#2	EVIL, INC.	#30	THE DEADLIEST DARE
#3	CULT OF CRIME	#31	WITHOUT A TRACE
#4	THE LAZARUS PLOT	#32	BLOOD MONEY
#5	EDGE OF DESTRUCTION	#33	COLLISION COURSE
#6	THE CROWNING TERROR	#34	FINAL CUT
#7	DEATHGAME	#35	THE DEAD SEASON
#8	SEE NO EVIL	#36	RUNNING ON EMPTY
#9	THE GENIUS THIEVES	#37	DANGER ZONE
#10	HOSTAGES OF HATE	#38	DIPLOMATIC DECEIT
#11	BROTHER AGAINST BROTHER	#39	FLESH AND BLOOD
#12	PERFECT GETAWAY	#40	FRIGHT WAVE
#13	THE BORGIA DAGGER	#41	HIGHWAY ROBBERY
#14	TOO MANY TRAITORS	#42	THE LAST LAUGH
#15	BLOOD RELATIONS	#43	STRATEGIC MOVES
#16	LINE OF FIRE	#44	CASTLE FEAR
#17	THE NUMBER FILE	#45	IN SELF-DEFENSE
#18	A KILLING IN THE MARKET	#46	FOUL PLAY
#19	NIGHTMARE IN ANGEL CITY	#47	FLIGHT INTO DANGER
#20	WITNESS TO MURDER	#48	ROCK 'N' REVENGE
#21	STREET SPIES	#49	DIRTY DEEDS
#22	DOUBLE EXPOSURE	#50	POWER PLAY
#23	DISASTER FOR HIRE	#51	CHOKE HOLD
#24	SCENE OF THE CRIME	#52	UNCIVIL WAR
#25	THE BORDERLINE CASE	#53	WEB OF HORROR
#26	TROUBLE IN THE PIPELINE	#54	DEEP TROUBLE
#27	NOWHERE TO RUN	#55	BEYOND THE LAW
#28	COUNTDOWN TO TERROR	#56	HEIGHT OF DANGER
		#57	TERROR ON TRACK
		#58	SPIKED!
		#59	OPEN SEASON
		#60	DEADFALL
		#61	GRAVE DANGER

Available from ARCHWAY Paperbacks

THE HARDY BOYS CASEFILES NO. 61

GRAVE DANGER

FRANKLIN W. DIXON

AN ARCHWAY PAPERBACK
Published by POCKET BOOKS
New York   London   Toronto   Sydney   Tokyo   Singapore

AN ARCHWAY PAPERBACK *Original*

An Archway Paperback published by
POCKET BOOKS, a division of Simon & Schuster Inc.
1230 Avenue of the Americas, New York, NY 10020

ISBN: 0-671-73097-5

First Archway Paperback printing March 1992

10 9 8 7 6 5 4 3 2 1

THE HARDY BOYS, AN ARCHWAY PAPERBACK
and colophon are registered trademarks of Simon & Schuster Inc.

THE HARDY BOYS CASEFILES is a trademark
of Simon & Schuster Inc.

Cover art by Brian Kotzky

Printed in the U.S.A.

IL 6+

Chapter

1

"I LOOK LIKE a penguin in this thing," eighteen-year-old Frank Hardy complained. He straightened his bow tie as he stepped onto the front porch of the Conrado mansion, outside of Bayport.

"Oh, come on, Frank. You look great," his girlfriend, Callie Shaw, said, complimenting him.

Frank shifted uncomfortably in his rented tuxedo once more and glared at the heavy paneled oak door looming before them. He knew this was going to be one of those boring grown-up parties, the kind his mom and aunt Gertrude were always trying to get him and his brother, Joe, to attend.

Frank smiled at Callie, deciding to make the best of a lousy situation. She smiled back and didn't seem at all uncomfortable being dressed up. In fact, she looked terrific.

Callie was wearing a green strapless dress in the unseasonably warm spring night air. Her blond hair was pulled back from her face to show off the dangling diamond earrings she had borrowed from her mother. In her heels she was taller than usual, only a few inches short of Frank's six foot one.

"I'm so excited!" Callie burst out.

"So am I," Frank said, forcing a grin.

She punched him on the arm. "Right. You're about as excited as Joe was."

"Wrong." Frank shook his head. "At least I showed up."

"Well, I appreciate it," Callie said. "Sometimes I don't understand your brother."

"In this case I do," Frank said. "He really hates getting dressed up, and since he knew Clint would be happy to take Renata—"

"Shhh," Callie said. "Here they come."

She nodded her head in the direction of Clint Herbert and Renata Walker, who had just parked the car they had driven to the party. The two of them were walking up the brick path to join Frank and Callie.

Renata, who was in their class at Bayport High, was wearing a silver sequined gown that glinted in sharp contrast to her ebony skin. She was tall and thin—almost six feet—but not as tall or thin as Clint. And on her, Frank thought, tall and thin looked good.

Clint, on the other hand, was built like a pencil. And in the old tuxedo he was wearing he resembled a chewed-up pencil. Even his thin red hair, which he'd carefully slicked back, was already falling forward over his eyes. He was a mess. Frank couldn't believe he was only a few years older than the rest of them and already a senior in college.

"Nice house, huh?" Clint said as he and Renata reached the front porch. "This probably cost a few bucks to build."

A few million of them, Frank thought as he rang the doorbell. He took a few steps back to peer at the huge bay windows on either side of the doorway and at the wooden railings and narrow porch that circled the entire second story. The house was huge. He guessed there were at least twenty rooms. From what he'd heard, the owner, Jorge Conrado, had the money to fill those rooms.

Frank turned his attention back to the front door just as it swung open.

A thin, balding man dressed in formal wear stood waiting in the doorway.

"Good evening. May I help you?" he inquired.

"Yes," Callie said, stepping forward. She handed him two parchment-colored envelopes. "We're here for the benefit party."

The butler nodded and took the envelopes

from Callie. They were the fanciest invitations Frank had ever seen. On the outside of each, written in gold script, were the words The Five Hundred.

That referred to the Bayport 500, the foundation created by the corporations and individuals that were sponsoring the party. Callie and Renata had received invitations because they had won scholarships from the 500 for special study programs during the coming summer. Frank and Clint were their escorts.

The butler handed the invitations back to Callie. "Ms. Shaw, Ms. Walker. If you and the gentlemen will follow me, please."

He stepped aside to let them pass.

After shutting the door behind them, he led the way into a house that was just as impressive inside as out. Frank caught a glimpse of a handsome paneled room filled with books on his left, and a formal sitting room on his right. They passed down a hallway with sculptures displayed in recessed alcoves on either side of them, like exhibits in a museum.

"A Mayan stela," Cliff whispered, pointing to an alcove that held a large gray stone with hieroglyphic symbols chiseled along its side. He pronounced the word "steel-uh." "Kind of like an ancient marker. We saw a lot of them on my dig last summer."

Clint was talking about the archaeological dig he'd been on in Mexico the year before. It, too, had been sponsored by the 500. The professor in charge of that dig was a man named Rafael Ortega. Ortega was now giving a seminar in archaeology at the university that Callie and Renata had been invited to take because of their scholarships. It met every two weeks.

At the far end of the hallway was a set of French doors. As they approached them, Frank could hear music and the rising buzz of conversation. The butler pushed the doors open.

More than two hundred people, all in formal attire, were standing outside on the huge, manicured back lawn. Some were drinking champagne from flute glasses. Some were dancing to the music from a full orchestra. Still others were eating from the twelve-foot buffet table.

Frank straightened his bow tie for the tenth time. The food didn't look bad. This might be all right.

The butler led them toward the center of the lawn and stopped in front of a circle of people busily engaged in conversation.

He waited for a pause. "Ms. Callie Shaw and Ms. Renata Walker, sir."

"Ah, yes. Thank you, Edward." A man dressed in black evening wear detached himself from the circle and stepped forward. He was tall and slender, with jet black hair slicked back against his temples, and looked to be in his late forties or early fifties.

"Welcome. I am Jorge Conrado," he said,

5

with just a trace of a Spanish accent. He smiled, revealing a mouthful of shiny white teeth, and shook hands with Callie and Renata. "You're this coming summer's scholarship winners, aren't you?"

"Yes, sir," Callie said, taking Frank's arm. "This is my escort, Frank Hardy."

"Pleased to meet you," Frank said, extending his hand. "This is a beautiful house, and it's a beautiful party."

"Thank you. I'm just pleased it was warm enough to be out of doors." Conrado turned to Clint next. "You, young man, look familiar."

Clint nodded. "Yes, sir. I'm Clint Herbert. I was on a dig last summer that the Five Hundred sponsored."

"Of course. At the Cobá site," Conrado said.

"Clint pointed out the stela you have in your hall," Frank added. "Are you interested in the Maya?"

"I am." Conrado's eyes brightened. "And you? Have you studied Mayan history?"

"A little," Frank said. Actually, he had only paged through some of the books Callie was studying for her seminar. "I really don't know much, though."

"There's a great deal no one knows," Conrado said, setting his glass down on a nearby table. "And yet they ruled an empire that lasted six times as long as that of the Romans."

"You're not giving your Mayan lecture again,

are you?'' A tall, elegant-looking woman who appeared to be about half Conrado's age stepped forward.

"It's no lecture, my darling,'' Conrado said, taking her arm and gently pulling her toward him. "These young people seem to be genuinely interested.'' He smiled. "Allow me to present my wife.''

"Stephanie,'' she said, shaking hands with each of them. "I'm pleased to meet you.'' She was model thin, with long black hair. Around her neck she wore a gold chain from which hung a huge medallion of carved jade.

Frank almost whistled out loud. Not only did the piece look expensive, it also looked very old. There were figures carved into it, though he couldn't make out what they were.

"Clint here was in Cobá last summer on the dig,'' Conrado said.

"Is that so?'' Stephanie said politely before changing the subject. "Well, you'll have to excuse my husband when he talks about the Maya. He's got Mexican blood in his veins.

"You all look too young to be part of any Five Hundred corporation,'' Stephanie continued. "So I can only assume you're students.''

"Yes, ma'am,'' Frank said. "We all go to Bayport High—except Clint. He's in college.''

"Are you studying the Maya in school, Clint?'' Conrado asked. He paused, waiting for an answer.

7

Clint hadn't heard. He was staring at Conrado's wife.

"Young man," Conrado prompted.

"What? Oh. Yes, yes sir, I am," Clint said, shaking his head as if to clear it. "I hope to go back to Mexico someday."

Just then the butler came up behind Conrado and whispered in his ear. "Please excuse us," the host said. He spread his arms expansively in the direction of the banquet table. "Help yourselves. We'll speak again later." Then Conrado and Stephanie disappeared into the crowd.

"Why were you staring at Conrado's wife?" Renata asked. "You seemed to be hypnotized."

"Because of that jade piece she was wearing," Clint said. "I've seen that medallion somewhere before."

"Why didn't you just ask her where it came from?" Callie said.

"I should have," Clint admitted. "But I was kind of flustered."

"Well," Frank said, "go ask them now."

"I don't want to monopolize their time."

"Maybe you could discuss the Cobá dig," Callie suggested.

Clint snapped his fingers. "That's it! The Cobá dig!" he said excitedly. "That's where I've seen the jade before!"

Without another word he strode purposefully across the lawn toward Conrado, his wife, and some others. Frank, Callie, and Renata followed a step behind him.

"Excuse me," Clint said, pointing at the jade medallion that hung from Stephanie's neck. "Could I please see that?"

"What seems to be the trouble?" Conrado said, obviously annoyed by the interruption but trying not to show it.

"Clint," Frank said, feeling guilty about telling Clint to talk to the Conrados. "Maybe we should—"

Clint shook his head. "The jade," he repeated. "Could I see it?"

Stephanie removed the chain and held it out to Clint, who began examining it immediately.

"Frank," Callie whispered in his ear. "What's he doing?"

Renata looked horrified. Her escort seemed to have gone a little bit crazy.

"This is it," Clint said, nodding vigorously to himself. "I know it."

"This is what?" Conrado said, an edge to his voice. "What are you talking about?"

"This piece. It's from the dig last summer. Professor Ortega said it was one of the most important pieces he'd ever found."

"I'm sure you're mistaken," Conrado said.

"No, sir." Clint shook his head emphatically. "I recognize the carvings. I'm positive."

"What are you saying, Clint?" Frank asked.

"I'm saying that this is a piece we found in

Mexico. Somehow it must have been stolen from the dig.''

''My medallion! Stolen?'' Stephanie appeared to be stunned, Conrado shocked.

''Frank, watch it!'' Callie yelled.

He turned just in time to catch Stephanie Conrado, who fainted dead away in his arms.

Chapter

2

BACK IN BAYPORT Frank's seventeen-year-old brother, Joe, was reading *Auto & Driver* magazine when he suddenly shouted, "A Tucker! Nobody told me Conrado had a Tucker!"

"What's that, dear?" Joe's aunt Gertrude asked from the sofa.

"Conrado. He owns a Tucker," Joe repeated.

"Conrado. Is he the boy who came over for lunch last week?"

Joe rolled his eyes. "No, Aunt Gertrude. He's the guy hosting the party Frank and Callie went to tonight. And he just happens to own one of the fifty remaining Tuckers in the world."

"What's a Tucker?" his aunt asked.

"It's a kind of car. It was built by a guy named Preston Tucker." He showed his aunt a picture of the car on the front cover of his magazine. "This was probably my only chance ever to get to see one."

Joe was now regretting his decision to skip out on the benefit. In fact, he'd been regretting it all night, he realized—especially after he had seen how good Renata looked when she and Clint had come by to pick Frank up.

Well, spring vacation had just started, and he and Frank were flying down to Fort Lauderdale, Florida, the day after tomorrow. There'd be plenty of girls there, for sure. Anyway, everyone knew that nothing exciting ever happened at those society parties.

Frank carried Stephanie to her room, where Conrado put her to bed. The others waited quietly in the hall for them.

"She'll be fine," Conrado said, rejoining them. "I think it was a combination of shock and the stress she's been under preparing for the party. What I don't understand, though, is how you can be so sure that this is the same piece of jade you found on the dig." As he spoke he held up Stephanie's necklace for them to see.

"You don't forget a discovery like that one, Mr. Conrado," Clint said. "It was the biggest find of the entire dig. We found the undisturbed tomb of a warrior-king called Cloud Ixmix, who lived back in the ninth century." Clint pointed to a series of carvings in the jade. "This is Ixmix's royal seal. I could never forget it. The professor figured this jade belonged to him, or at least to one of his high priests."

Frank leaned forward so he could see better. The piece was about eight inches long, and at the top of it were two seated men with headdresses, facing each other. Between the two figures was what appeared to be a bird—an owl, he saw now. It probably had something to do with Mayan religious beliefs.

"I've seen pictures of that seal as well, Mr. Conrado," Callie said. "Professor Ortega showed us slides of the dig in our class. That looks like the same piece."

Conrado frowned. "This is very serious then." He remained silent a moment, his brows creased in thought.

"You bet," Clint said. "That medallion should be in a museum somewhere in Mexico."

Frank nodded. He knew that Mexico had one of the toughest laws in the world about keeping its national treasures safe. There was no way a piece like the one Clint was describing would ever have been allowed out of the country.

"First we have to make sure that this is genuine," Frank began. "It could be just a replica. We should call Professor Ortega and ask him to check it out."

"You're right," Callie said. "The professor will know in a minute if the piece is genuine."

Conrado nodded. "An excellent suggestion."

"We could try him at the university," Clint said. "Sometimes he works late."

Frank noticed a phone sitting on an antique table next to the bedroom door.

"Do you mind, Mr. Conrado?" he asked.

"Not at all."

"Here, Clint," Frank said, picking up the receiver. "You should call. He knows you best."

Clint quickly punched in the professor's number at the university. He held the receiver up to his ear for a few seconds before setting it down. "No answer. But I can call him at home."

Frank decided that if Ortega was as dedicated to his work as Callie had told him, he surely wouldn't mind being bothered at home for this.

"That's strange," Clint said, hanging up the phone after trying Ortega's home phone. "The number's been disconnected."

"Let's call the professor's graduate assistant," Renata suggested.

Conrado glanced at his watch and frowned. "I need to get back to my guests, but please let me know the minute you find out anything."

Frank nodded and followed their host back to the stairs, watching as he made his way down them. A half dozen people were waiting at the bottom for him, all clearly worried.

"I hope we haven't ruined the party," Callie said, quietly coming up behind him and taking his hand.

"Well, we've obviously upset Mrs. Conrado,

14

but I think everything will turn out okay." Frank was now betting that Clint was wrong about the piece being the same one that Professor Ortega had found on the dig.

As Frank and Callie started walking back to Clint and Renata, Frank heard Clint start talking to someone on the phone. Maybe he'd gotten through to someone who could find Ortega. "I really do think everything will be all right once we clear up the mystery of the jade."

"Mystery?" Callie said, staring at him closely.

Frank had to smile. He and his brother *were* always getting involved in mysteries, but not this time. He hadn't even asked Conrado where he had got the medallion.

"I'm not getting involved," he protested. "Don't forget, Joe and I leave for Florida in a couple of days. It's really too bad you can't come with us," he said.

"I know," Callie said. "But my folks planned our camping trip a long time ago. Besides, it'll be fun to get away with them." She looked closely at Frank and smiled. "Really. A lot of fun."

He smiled back. "Right."

They both burst out laughing.

"I hope this turns out to be a case for you. I hope Ortega comes here tomorrow and says that the piece is genuine! Then you and Joe will have to cancel your trip to sunny Florida."

"I don't think Professor Ortega will be coming

here tomorrow," Renata interrupted, coming up behind them with Clint. They both looked very upset. "I just got off the phone with Andre, the professor's graduate assistant. Yesterday he went to visit Ortega to give him some papers he'd graded."

"But when he got to the professor's office," Clint continued, "he found a lot of his stuff was gone. Finally he tracked down the department chairman, who swore him to secrecy. It took me ten minutes to convince Andre this was important enough to let us in on what's going on."

"What is it? Has something happened to the professor?" Callie asked.

"You could say that," Clint said. "I think he's been framed."

"Framed?" Frank shook his head. Maybe this was going to turn out to be a mystery after all. "Framed for what?"

"For something he didn't do!" Clint said, suddenly angry. "Something he would never do in a million years!"

"Well, if he's so innocent, why did he take off without telling anyone?" Renata asked. "Tell me that."

"I don't know," Clint said. He waved one of his long, thin arms in a dismissive gesture. "But when we find him, I'm sure he'll have a good reason."

"Hold on a second," Frank said. He raised

his hands. "Time out. Just tell us what happened to the professor."

"Well, that's just it. We don't know." Renata sighed heavily. "Nobody knows where he is."

"And here's the ridiculous thing," Clint said. He paused, his gaze meeting Frank's and holding it. "He's suspected of stealing the stuff we found in Mexico last summer, smuggling it into the country, and selling it to collectors here."

Chapter

3

"I DON'T BELIEVE IT, either," Callie said. "I *can't* believe it. He always talks about how important the past is, especially for countries like Mexico, which have had so much stolen before."

"Whoa," Frank said, holding up a hand again. "Slow down. Clint, tell me why they think Ortega's guilty."

"Let's get Mr. Conrado first, so I won't have to repeat the story," Clint suggested.

Renata returned shortly with Mr. Conrado, and the group assembled in the paneled room Frank had seen when he first entered the house. There was a huge, detailed map of the world on one wall, and the wall opposite it was taken up almost entirely with bookshelves, which Conrado was standing in front of now.

"The Mexican officials phoned the university the day before yesterday. They said Ortega's dig records didn't match theirs," Clint began. "They say it looks as if he found some way to keep about half of what he found."

"Is he going to be arrested?" Callie asked worriedly.

Clint shook his head. "They can't even find him, so obviously they can't arrest him. Also, there's no actual proof yet. The Mexican authorities only contacted the university to let them know about their problem."

Frank was very confused. How could a college professor have expected to get away with something like this? Why would the authorities contact the university? Because they couldn't reach the professor? Why did the professor disappear? He must have heard about the phone call, Frank decided. It was the only thing that made sense.

Conrado slowly shook his head. "This could be very bad for the Five Hundred." He gazed at the four of them. "Something like this could set the entire foundation back years. I'd appreciate it if the four of you would keep quiet about this until the matter is settled."

"Smuggling isn't the kind of thing that goes away, sir," Frank warned him. "Sooner or later it will come out."

"I prefer it to be later," Conrado replied

firmly. "After we find out exactly what happened."

"Your wife's jade really could be the piece they discovered on the dig, then," Frank pointed out. "I've been wanting to ask how you found it and where."

"I purchased it—at a gallery called Xavier Antiques, in New York City. Many of my pieces have come from there." Conrado shook his head. "If they're smuggled as well—"

"There's no need to worry about that yet, sir," Frank said.

"Well, I'll just have to see about that," Conrado said. "And now I have to get back to my guests once again." He left the room, closing the door behind him.

"Frank," Callie said after Conrado left, "I want you to do me a favor. Please find out what happened on that dig."

"What?" He shook his head. "Callie, that'd be impossible at this point. I'd have to go to Mexico, talk to the authorities, find out who Ortega had with him on the dig, find out what they found, what they might not have turned in. . . ."

"All right, I get the picture." She frowned. "But couldn't you at least check out that gallery Conrado mentioned? The one his wife's jade medallion came from?"

"Xavier Antiques?"

She nodded. "It is right in New York, you

know. And you and Joe are going to be there tomorrow, anyway."

He couldn't argue with that. He and his brother had planned on spending their first day of spring break in New York City before they flew out the next morning. Still, he wasn't sure what good going to the antique shop would do. He doubted that the people there would admit to selling stolen merchandise.

"What am I going to do there?"

Callie shook her head. "I don't know. You're the detective. I'm sure you'll think of something."

Frank frowned.

"Please," Callie said. "It's important to me."

"All right. I'll do it, but just for you." He sighed and got to his feet. "Let's go see if they have any food left. And I'd better bring something back for Joe, too. How else am I going to convince him to spend the first day of his vacation working?"

"No way," Joe said, shaking his head. He couldn't believe it. Not only had Frank interrupted the last five minutes of the horror movie by coming home early, now he wanted them to start working the day before they left for Florida.

"Relax," Frank said. "It's only a little errand."

"Sure," Joe said. "These things start out as one little errand, then before you know it—bam!

It's like when Mom asks me to pick up something from the store. Next thing I know I'm carrying a bag full of toilet paper and vegetables."

"I promise, Joe," Frank said. "All we'll do is look at the gallery."

Joe shook his head. *"You* look at the gallery. I'll wait outside."

"Okay," Frank said. He tossed a book at Joe. "You can read this while you're waiting."

Joe looked at the cover. *The Mayas*. By Gilbert De Camp."

"I borrowed it from Callie," Frank said. "You can bone up on authentic Mayan artifacts while I find out how much Professor Ortega sold them for—if he did."

"Oh, come on, Frank, have a heart," Joe pleaded. "This is work. We're supposed to be going on vacation."

"We are. We're just going to take a little detour first."

"Sure," Joe said. He examined the food Frank had brought home from the party. It actually looked good. He grabbed a sandwich out of the bag and took a big bite.

It was good.

"All right," he decided. "I'll do it."

"You're all heart," Frank said. He got up from the chair, barely dodging the pillow Joe threw. "I'm going to bed."

"Good night." Joe settled back on the couch

and turned on the TV again. Another horror movie was just starting.

He wondered how those little sandwiches would taste heated up.

"Train food," Joe said, sitting next to his brother. He unwrapped the hamburger he'd bought from the food-service car and stared at it. "Yecchh."

"If you hadn't stayed up so late, you could have gotten an early start," Frank said. "And a real breakfast."

"Worms get early starts," Joe said. "People don't have to."

"If they want to catch a train and get breakfast at home, they do."

"Next stop, New York City," the train conductor announced. "Please check the overhead baggage rack and your seats for your personal belongings."

Joe watched as his brother began gathering up their things. He handed Frank the book on the Maya, which he had started reading on the trip in from Bayport.

He'd been fascinated. The Maya were perfecting astronomical calendars and agriculture while Europe was in the middle of the Dark Ages. They'd built cities all through Central America's Yucatán peninsula, cities with names like Chichén Itzá, Copan, and Tulum. There was even a short chapter on Cobá in the book, which made it sound like a pretty exciting place to visit. Joe hoped he'd get there someday.

The train came to a stop, and people began squeezing out the doors. Joe followed Frank through the terminal to a subway station. They caught a train downtown and emerged onto lower Broadway just as Frank's watch beeped, signaling twelve noon. It could have been early evening, the sky was so cloudy and gray.

"All right," Joe said. "Where is this Xavier Antiques?"

"The address," Frank said, reading from a piece of paper he'd pulled out of his pocket, "is Five Parsons Place." He pointed to a sign across the street. "There."

Parsons turned out to be a quiet side street, and number five was an old five-story brownstone with a sign above the first floor that said Xavier Antiques. But the iron gates in front of the windows were padlocked shut.

"That's weird." Joe looked through the bars at the sign indicating the gallery's hours. "They're supposed to open at eleven today."

"I guess we should have phoned ahead." Frank stood beside him and peered through the glass. "It looks deserted in there."

"Come on," Joe said. "Maybe there's another entrance."

Frank followed him as he jogged around the right side of the building and down the alley next to it, stopping at a delivery entrance sign. The sign was above a short flight of stairs that led down to a heavy metal door. Joe crept down, turned the knob, and the door swung open.

"Do we go in?" he asked.

Frank hesitated but only for a second. "We came to check out anything suspicious. I'd say an unlocked shop qualifies, wouldn't you?"

Joe had started forward into the dark room when he noticed a thin wire hanging down from the doorframe. "The burglar alarm's been disconnected."

"And by an expert," Frank said. "We'd better be careful."

Joe nodded and looked around. He was standing in a huge space—some kind of storage area, judging from the crates scattered everywhere. He switched on a single bulb hanging in the far corner of the room. It provided just enough light to see by.

"Up there," Frank said, pointing toward a flight of stairs about twenty feet ahead of them.

Joe nodded and started climbing. Were they about to surprise a burglar? He hoped there was another explanation for the disconnected alarm.

When he reached the door at the top of the stairs Joe paused and listened. "I don't hear anything," he whispered, turning back to Frank. "I'm going in."

"Careful," his brother warned. Joe stepped out and found himself in the middle of what must have been the selling area. Now, though, it was empty. There was just enough light shining in through the iron gates to see that the display cases lining the walls were empty.

"Either our burglar is a fast worker, or this place is closed down," Joe whispered. He walked up to one display case and ran a finger along the edge. It came away clean. "And pretty recently—no more than a few days ago."

"Hey," Frank said, pointing behind Joe. "Look."

Joe turned and saw a doorway on the far side of the room. There was a light coming from underneath it.

"Our burglar," Frank whispered. "Let's—"

The light under the door suddenly clicked off.

Holding a finger to his lips, Frank grabbed his brother's arm and pointed toward one side of the wall flanking the door. Joe nodded and stole across the floor quickly to take up his position there, while Frank flattened himself against the wall on the other side of the door.

The door to the room swung open, and a man stepped out. As he started to pass him, Joe tapped him on the shoulder.

"What the—" The intruder tried to throw a punch at Joe, who blocked the blow easily with one arm. Frank came up behind the man, grabbed his arms, and pinned them behind his back. The intruder twisted about furiously, struggling to free himself.

"Let me go," the man said. He spoke with a slight Spanish accent. "I haven't done anything!"

"The police might disagree with you," Frank pointed out. "You jimmied the lock downstairs and disconnected the burglar alarm."

"I did nothing of the sort. That door was unlocked when I got here."

Joe frowned, studying the intruder more closely. He was older, probably in his late forties, with a full beard and longish graying hair. He had on a brown cardigan sweater and jeans, hardly the kind of clothes a burglar wore.

"And as for disconnecting the burglar alarm, I'd have no idea how to do that. I'm a college professor, not a thief."

Joe's eyes widened. College professor? Joe knew his brother was thinking the same thing.

"Check him," Frank said.

Joe reached into the intruder's back pocket and pulled out his wallet. Every piece of ID identified the man as Rafael Ortega.

"It's him," Joe nodded, putting the wallet back. Frank let the man go. "We've got a lot of questions for you, Professor."

"Hold it." His brother held up a hand. "Did you hear anything?"

Joe cocked his head a moment, listening. All he heard were the sounds of traffic from the street outside. "No. Did you?"

Frank nodded, turning to Ortega. "Did you come here alone?"

"Yes, and I can assure you there's no one else here. I've been inside for almost a half hour."

Now Joe heard the noise—footsteps behind him. He whirled around.

A man was standing in the shadows next to one of the empty display cases.

"And what exactly were you looking for, Professor?" the newcomer asked. "Artifacts, maybe? Like the ones you had smuggled out of Mexico?"

Joe had the sinking feeling they'd just found the man who had disconnected the burglar alarm.

"You know you left the door unlocked downstairs," Joe said. "That's not smart, not in this neighborhood—"

"Shut up, kid," the man said, stepping forward. Now that he was out of the shadows Joe could see the gun in his hand. He held it with the practiced ease of a professional and had it leveled right at them.

"I'll do the talking around here."

Chapter

4

FRANK TENSED. If he could distract the gunman for a second—

"Whatever you're thinking, don't."

Another man stepped forward from behind the door at the top of the stairs, where he'd apparently been hiding the whole time. He had a gun in his hand, too.

Frank wanted to kick himself. He felt like an amateur, getting ambushed this way. He and Joe didn't usually make those kinds of mistakes.

"Who are you two kids?" the first man asked. "And what are you doing here?"

"Why should we tell you anything?" Frank asked, deciding to take the offensive.

The man smiled and pointed at his gun. "You figure it out."

Frank decided the gun was a good enough reason. "My name is Frank Hardy. That's my brother, Joe."

"Is that supposed to mean something?" The gunman shook his head. "I've never heard of you."

"I wouldn't try anything funny if I were you," Joe warned. "People know we're here."

Somehow Frank didn't think that was going to do them a lot of good right at that moment.

"Don't worry, kid," the first man said. To Frank's surprise, he holstered his gun. "We're not going to hurt anybody. We just want to ask you some questions."

"What for?" Frank frowned. "Who are you guys?"

"Yes," Ortega repeated. "Who are you?"

The man reached into his coat and pulled out a wallet-size leather case. As he flipped the case open the low light glinted on something inside. A badge. Frank moved closer and read the insignia.

"Treasury Department?"

"That's right." The man nodded. "Agent Richards. Hunt Richards. And this is my partner, Agent Andrews."

Joe frowned. "You disconnected the burglar alarm downstairs? And unlocked the door?" He shook his head. "Why?"

"Wait a minute. What are treasury agents doing in an antiques shop in New York City?"

Frank asked, though he suspected he knew the answer already. The Treasury Department was the government agency charged with stopping smuggling.

"Five days ago, on a tip from the Mexican authorities, we intercepted a shipment of pottery bound for this place. Only it wasn't just pottery we found inside the crates." Richards stared at Ortega. "There were six artifacts that we positively identified as coming from a dig in Mexico last summer. But I guess I'm not telling you anything new, am I, Professor?"

Ortega's face turned scarlet. "I have nothing to do with smugglers."

"Oh, really?" Richards asked sarcastically. "Then what, may I ask, are you doing here?"

"The same thing you are," the professor declared fiercely. "I'm trying to find out who stole my discoveries!"

"Or do you just want the money they owe you?" Andrews put in.

"Money they owe me?" Ortega seemed genuinely puzzled. "What on earth are you talking about?"

"He means the money the smugglers paid you for your artifacts," Frank said, suddenly feeling very sorry for the professor. The shipment of pottery, coupled with Ortega's appearance here, was pretty convincing evidence. But then, too, it was all circumstantial. He remembered the promise he'd made to Callie to try to find out what had really happened on the dig. Just as suddenly, another idea occurred to him.

"Agent Richards," he began, "I have a suggestion."

"Stay out of this, kid." The man waved him off. "What do you say, Professor? A little cooperation now might go a long way toward reducing your sentence."

Ortega folded his arms across his chest. "I have nothing further to say to you."

"Look, Professor," Richards said, leaning back against a display case, "we've got you for trespassing. We know you stole pieces from your dig, and we also know you haven't gotten paid for them yet. Your bank balance hasn't changed in a year. Now, why don't you make it easy on yourself. Tell us who smuggled the pieces into this country."

Ortega just shook his head and remained silent.

"Agent Richards," Frank tried again. "If I could just say something—"

"Quiet, kid!" he barked, and continued to glare at Ortega. "We're not really interested in you, Professor. We're after the person with the money and the contacts to smuggle those treasures out of Mexico and into the hands of private American collectors. We know this place was used as a clearinghouse for the stuff, and that they used you to get it out of the site safely. But beyond that . . .'' He shrugged.

Ortega's eyes blazed. "All right. I will tell you something, Agent Richards," he said.

Richards leaned forward. "I'm all ears, Professor."

"You," Ortega said slowly, punctuating each word with a jab of his index finger, "are an idiot. I had nothing to do with any smuggling! Nothing! And that's my final word on the subject!"

"That's it," Richards said, tight lipped. He grabbed Ortega by the arm. "Let's go. Maybe a night in jail will jog your memory."

"Agent Richards, wait!" Frank said, talking as fast as he could before Richards cut him off again. "You don't have any proof against the professor, so what if I work with him to find out who's behind the smuggling ring? Will you agree to drop the charges against Professor Ortega?"

Richards's mouth fell open. For that matter, so did Joe's, but Frank was less concerned about his brother right then.

"I must be crazy," the treasury agent said. "Could you repeat that?"

Frank did. Richards just shook his head.

"That's the nuttiest proposition I've ever heard, kid," he said. "Why in the world would I even consider it?"

Frank smiled. "Hold on. Let me make one or two phone calls."

* * *

By six that evening Frank and Joe were at their hotel next to Kennedy Airport, having a fast-food supper with Professor Ortega.

Richards had actually agreed to Frank's proposal after a man high up in a secret government agency called the Network and Fenton Hardy, Frank's father, vouched for the boys. Fenton had had a long and distinguished career in the New York Police Department and was now a world-famous private investigator. When Frank had put him on the phone with Richards, Fenton had been able to convince the treasury agent that his sons were worth trusting. Especially when it turned out that Fenton Hardy was good friends with Richards's boss.

"All right, Professor," Frank said, pushing aside his tray. "Let's start at the beginning. What really happened at Cobá last summer?"

"Nothing out of the ordinary. That's why this is all so puzzling to me." The professor took a big gulp of water from his glass and wiped his lips. "The dig was a spectacular success. Once we found Cloud Ixmix's tomb we had more press coverage than we could handle. The Mexican government had representatives on the site daily, helping us catalog the artifacts we found." He shrugged. "Now they say half those artifacts never made it to their storage areas."

"Who else had access to the artifacts?" Frank asked.

"Dozens of people, but I knew almost all of

them. I'd have trouble believing any of them were involved in this." He sighed and picked up his tray. "I'm going to get another cup of coffee," he said, standing. "If you'll excuse me."

"One little errand," Joe said when Ortega was out of earshot. "That's what you told me. Okay, Frank. I understand you're not going to Florida with me. You promised Richards you'd help Ortega, and obviously you can't do that in one night. But you're not keeping me from going."

"I wouldn't think of it—I promise. You're just in a bad mood because we didn't go to a pizza place," he said.

"Don't try to change the subject," Joe told him. "I've got until seven o'clock tomorrow morning, when my plane for Florida leaves, to help you. But at seven o'clock I'll be officially on vacation."

"I understand that," Frank said.

"Good." Joe settled back in his chair. "So do you think Ortega's telling the truth?"

"I don't know," Frank admitted. "I was telling Callie what he said at the antiques shop—"

"You talked to Callie?" Joe interrupted. "When?"

"While you and the professor were checking in," Frank told him. "She says hello."

"Who says hello?" Ortega asked, returning with his coffee.

"Callie. She wanted me to say hi to you, too.

35

"What about the Mexican police?" Joe asked, getting back to more pressing business. "Who do they suspect is involved in stealing the artifacts?"

"Besides me, you mean? I don't know. I never actually spoke to them. I cleared out before they contacted me." Ortega shook his head. "They're worse than the U.S. Treasury Department agents." He slammed his hand down on the table. Coffee splashed over the side of his cup and onto the tray. "I have to go to Mexico to find out what's happened there! But I don't expect that fool Richards will let me leave the country, he's so convinced I'm the smuggler."

"I may be able to help you there," Frank said.

Both Joe and the professor turned to him at once.

"I talked to Richards again while you and Joe were checking in. I think he'll let you go." That was the other phone call he'd made, after speaking with Callie.

"Then I must book a flight immediately," Ortega said, standing again. "Frank, I can't thank you enough."

"That is, he'll let you go under certain conditions—if I accompany you."

"Wait a minute, Frank," Joe said. "Are you saying you don't want me to go with you?"

Frank turned to his brother and returned the

grin he saw on Joe's face. "Are you saying you *will* go?"

"You know I never could say no to a mystery," Joe replied.

"I don't understand," Ortega said. "What are you two talking about?"

"Sorry, Professor," Frank said. "I'll make it clearer. If you want," he continued—and even if you don't want, he added silently, remembering the deal he'd made with Richards—"we'll go with you to Mexico tomorrow to help track down the smugglers."

A huge grin broke out on the professor's face. "That would be wonderful. But how will I get into Mexico? I'm wanted for questioning."

"Richards and I decided no one would ever guess you'd go back to Mexico now—they won't even be on the lookout for you," Frank answered.

Frank wasn't too worried about keeping Ortega out of the hands of the authorities. But there was one ugly thought that kept nagging at him.

What if Ortega turned out to be one of the smugglers after all?

Chapter

5

JOE SMILED, TOO. Actually, he was glad to be going to Mexico.

If he was going to get involved, there were a few things he needed to know, though. "Professor," he said, "I have a question. What brought you to Xavier Antiques today?"

The grin disappeared from Ortega's face. He'd make a lousy smuggler, Joe decided. One look at him and you'd know exactly what he was thinking.

"I have to go back a few weeks to answer that," Ortega said. "To when I first became aware that something was wrong. A good friend of mine in Mexico called me. She said that there was a problem. The Department of Antiquities had found that a lot of the pieces from the Cobá

38

dig were missing. I asked her to keep me informed.

"My friend called me again this week. She told me that the government was going to round up everybody connected with the dig for questioning. That was when I decided to split. She also asked me if I'd heard of Xavier Antiques. She said they were known in the black market as a good place to unload stolen antiques.

"So I went there to look around. I went three times, but the place was never open. Then today I found that unlocked side door and went in. But there was nothing there. The office was as empty as the gallery." He shrugged. "The rest you know."

"Is the black market in antiquities big?" Frank asked.

"Tremendous," Ortega said. "You have no idea how much money some pieces sell for." He shook his head. "Private collectors pay millions of dollars for a piece that they end up hiding in the basement. I don't understand the attraction of that."

Joe did. The professor was just hanging out with the wrong crowd. In their cases, he and Frank had seen plenty of people who lived just to acquire possessions.

"I'm going to get a cup of coffee, too," Joe said, standing.

"You don't usually drink coffee," Frank said.

"I do when I have to stay up late."

"You're staying up late tonight? What for?" Frank frowned. "Don't get any ideas about watching late-night horror movies on cable in our room. I need to get a good night's sleep."

"Nope. No horror movies tonight." He smiled. "I want to finish reading the book that you gave me on the Maya."

"This volume is just a primer," Ortega said, holding up the book Joe had finished late the night before. "To really understand Mayan civilization you must visit the jungle."

Joe nodded sleepily and yawned, studying the tray full of airplane food in front of him. Despite a cup of coffee, he felt exhausted. He'd even slept through the in-flight movie.

He was sitting in the center section of the plane, while Frank and Ortega had seats directly across the aisle from him on the plane's left-hand side. Beside the professor, through the window of the airplane, Joe could see huge clouds, like giant beds of fluffy white pillows. He felt like climbing out the window and lying down on top of them.

"The jungle is a savage place," the professor continued. "And the Maya were a savage civilization. All of their achievements, their pyramids, their cities, their great roads, were built on the blood and sacrifice of a large slave population."

"That's true of a lot of ancient civilizations,

isn't it?'' Frank asked. ''The Egyptians, the Greeks, the Romans?''

Joe put down his fork. As far as he was concerned, his lunch had been uneatable. It was some sort of unidentifiable refried bean and meat combination.

''Yes, but none of them sacrificed quite as''— the professor paused, searching for the right word—''enthusiastically as the Maya.''

''I read about that in the book,'' Joe said as he passed the flight attendant his tray. ''They used those giant wells—''

''Cenotes,'' Ortega interrupted. He pronounced the word ''say-note-ees.'' ''They're present at almost every major Mayan site, though we never found one at Cobá.'' He frowned. ''They're a rich source of artifacts for archaeologists because so many victims were thrown into the wells wearing gold jewelry and the like, as offerings to the gods.''

''Probably a great place for smugglers to go, too,'' Joe said, instantly regretting his choice of words when he saw Ortega flush red.

''Sorry about that, Professor,'' he said weakly.

''No need to apologize,'' Ortega said. ''I expect I'll be hearing far worse when we reach Cancún.''

Joe checked his watch. Their flight was due into Mexico in less than half an hour.

''Cancún's a big tourist town, isn't it?'' he asked. ''I remember reading about it in a magazine." Actually, the article had made the place look a lot like Florida. Sun, sand, and girls in bikinis.

"The peninsula outside the city is. It's filled with big ugly American hotels and American restaurants," Ortega said with a snort. "Cancún itself is rather charming, actually. There are wonderful restaurants."

Joe nodded and yawned again. "I'm going for a walk," he announced. "I need to stretch my legs."

He headed down the aisle toward the rear of the plane, dreaming about Florida and what might have been.

He reached the back of the plane, turned, and started marching to the front.

Still, Cancún should be fun—when they weren't working. He remembered that the nightlife there was supposed to be incredible. The article he'd read said people stayed out dancing all night and slept on the beach all day. He could see it now . . .

Someone grabbed his arm.

"Excuse me, sir." It was a flight attendant. "You can't be in here. This is first class." She slid past him carrying an open bottle of champagne.

Sure enough, he'd accidentally wandered into the front of the plane. Before him he saw the door to the cockpit and the ten or so rows of luxury seats that made up first class. Whoops. That's what he got for daydreaming.

"Sorry," he said. He started to turn around but bumped right into a girl who had come up behind him. She dropped the stack of magazines she was carrying on his foot.

"Why don't you watch where you're going?" she snapped.

"Sorry," Joe mumbled again, but this time for a different reason.

The girl was beautiful.

"What are you staring at?" she demanded. "You want an autograph or something?"

Joe blinked. "An autograph?" He looked at her again, a couple of inches shy of six feet, thin, long brown hair, flawless skin, a beauty mark on the left side of her face, and he began to get a little angry. He couldn't stand people who thought being beautiful entitled them to be arrogant. He shook his head.

"No, I don't want an autograph," he said. "Who do you think you are, Madonna?"

"What?" Now she was mad. "You wish, you geek." She glared at him, and with those words brushed past him, leaving the magazines in a pile on the floor.

"What a jerk," Joe said.

"What's going on here?" the flight attendant asked. She saw Joe and the stack of magazines on the floor.

"That girl"—he pointed at her so the atten-

dant could see who he was talking about—
"walked right into me."

"Don't you know who that is?" the woman asked, eyes wide. "That's Ronnie Lane!"

"Who?" Joe asked.

"Ronnie Lane. The model!" The flight attendant bent down to pick up the magazines, and Joe leaned over to help her. "She's in all the Glamouresse ads."

"Well, I never heard of her," Joe said.

"I hope you didn't make her angry," the attendant said, casting a worried glance toward the beautiful young woman. "We don't want to upset her manager. Now please"—she gently turned Joe around—"take your seat. We're landing soon."

"What was all the commotion?" Frank asked as Joe sat down and buckled his seat belt.

"Nothing," he grumbled. "Just ran into some girl who thought she was Madonna or something."

Frank eyed him strangely as the captain announced they were beginning their descent into Cancún's airport.

For the first time during the flight Joe wished he had a window seat. From the few glimpses of scenery he caught through Ortega's window, it really looked like jungle down there.

Joe was the first of his group out of the airplane. The flight crew had wheeled a set of old-fashioned stairs up to the plane. He stood on the landing at the top for a moment, taking in his surroundings and the heat of the Mexican afternoon. After the air-conditioned chill of the last few hours the warm breeze coming in off the ocean was a relief.

"Welcome to spring break," Joe said, spreading out his arms. The airport was smaller than he had expected, considering that Cancún was a major tourist city. There were maybe half a dozen gates and two single landing strips. The terminal was a single building no bigger than Bayport High, but the scenery was spectacular.

Joe had spent a lot of time in the forests of New England, but he'd never seen anything as lush and green as the jungle around the airport. Even from a distance it felt different. More primitive. He found himself hoping that Cancún wouldn't be like Florida moved farther south. And even if it was, maybe they wouldn't have to spend a lot of time in the city. Cobá was in the middle of the jungle, after all. In fact, if the airport was any indication, no place around there would be too far from the jungle. Joe jogged quickly to the bottom of the stairs.

"Wow," Frank said, shielding his eyes from the sun with one hand as he made his way out the door. "That jungle looks spectacular." He turned to Ortega, who was a couple of steps behind him.

The professor smiled and opened his mouth to answer Frank.

Suddenly Frank heard a loud crack! Ortega made a gasping noise and stumbled forward into his arms. The unexpected weight sent Frank reeling and almost caused him to stumble backward down the stairs.

"What the—" he began.

People began to scream all around him. One woman who'd been immediately in front of Frank fell a couple of steps before catching herself. Joe looked up and heard shouts of anger and confusion. Somewhere a baby started crying.

For a second, Frank didn't know what had happened. Then he noticed the growing red stain on the back of Ortega's shirt.

"Somebody get a doctor!" he yelled. A flight attendant pushed her way to their side, shock spreading across her face.

"Hurry!" Joe said to her. "This man's been shot!"

Chapter

6

"THE CAPTAIN!" Frank yelled, struggling to be heard over the chaos. "Ask him to use the plane's radio to call for an ambulance!"

The flight attendant nodded, and Frank watched as Joe shoved his way back up the stairs to him and Ortega. Joe helped Frank lower Ortega slowly to the landing at the top of the stairs. He cradled the professor's head in his lap.

Ortega's eyes were glazing over. He gazed up at Joe and mumbled something indistinct.

"You've been shot, Professor. But you're going to be okay," Joe said. At least he hoped so. The bullet had struck Ortega squarely in the left shoulder. The biggest danger now was loss of blood. "Help is on the way."

"What's going on?" the flight attendant

asked, returning to them. "Why would anybody shoot him?"

Joe shook his head. Could it have anything to do with the smuggling? he wondered. That was the only explanation that made any sense. Whether or not Ortega was involved with the people who had stolen the Cobá artifacts, they might have good reason not to want him snooping around.

But how had they known what plane he would be on?

He stared down at the people milling about at the bottom of the stairs, most of whom were pointing upward. One of the flight attendants was trying to clear the area around the stairway. Uniformed men and women were rushing toward the plane from the gate area.

And far across the runway Joe could see a single figure sprinting toward the jungle. The gunman, maybe? It was worth finding out.

"Stay with the professor," he told Frank, scrambling to his feet. An ambulance sounded just then.

Joe vaulted over the railing on the side of the stair platform. He couldn't waste time trying to push past the officials making their way up the stairway. Holding on to the rail with one hand, he leapt down the outside of the stairs two at a time, his eyes never leaving the figure far ahead of him on the runway.

The man was about halfway to the jungle. If

he allowed him to reach it, Joe knew he would lose him.

He began to run past the crowd gathered at the bottom of the stairs and toward the jungle. His arms and legs were pumping like pistons.

The man glanced back and happened to see him. Joe noticed he was carrying something in his right hand. The rifle, maybe? He wasn't close enough to tell, not yet. He was gaining ground, but probably not fast enough. The man was going to reach the jungle long before Joe got to him.

A luggage cart came zooming down the runway, cutting directly across his line of pursuit.

"Hey, stop!" Joe called out, grabbing on to the roof of the cart as it shot past. He jumped up and planted one foot on the cart's floor and leaned in to talk to the driver. "I need your cart!" he shouted.

"Qué?" The man started, surprise on his face. *"Qué quiere usted?"* The driver's face now registered panic. A name tag on his shirt identified him as Eduardo.

"I need your cart!" Joe said again, wishing he could think of how to say it in Spanish. The driver began shouting at him in Spanish.

There just wasn't time to argue. With his free hand Joe gave the driver a hard shove, breaking the man's grip on the steering wheel and sliding him along the front seat. Then Joe swung into the driver's seat and spun the wheel, heading the cart in the direction of the gunman.

"Sorry about this, Ed, but that guy just shot my friend!" Joe shouted, his eyes firmly on the gunman, who was about five hundred feet in front of him. He hoped the driver would understand from his tone of voice that something important was going on.

Apparently, however, the only thing the driver understood was that some crazy kid had hijacked his cart. He continued shouting in rapid-fire Spanish, gesturing emphatically. Joe tried to ignore him and concentrate on the gunman, whom they were closing in on fast.

Just then the man glanced over his shoulder, catching sight of the cart. He was young, not much older than twenty-one or twenty-two, with bronzed skin and what could have been the beginnings of a mustache. That was a rifle he was carrying, Joe saw.

Suddenly the gunman stopped running, turned, and fired at them.

Joe didn't have enough warning to turn the cart. There was a loud clang as one shot hit the metal grille of the vehicle. A second shattered the windshield and buried itself in the cushioned seat between Joe and Eduardo. With a yowl, the driver threw himself out of the side of the cart.

Ahead of him, Joe saw the gunman raise his rifle again.

He slammed on the brakes and spun the wheel

hard to his left. There was a loud squealing sound and a yell from someone somewhere behind him, and he felt the cart begin to spin out of control. In that split second he realized that there was only a thin roof of canvas above him. If the car flipped over, he'd almost certainly be crushed!

Acting almost instinctively, he jammed his foot down on the accelerator again. The cart shot forward, easing out of its spin.

Suddenly there was a loud explosion. Joe thought he'd been shot at again. Then the cart began to wobble, and Joe knew he'd blown a tire. He brought the vehicle to a stop and climbed out, disgusted.

The right rear tire was completely flat. It looked as though it had been shot off. He slammed his hand against the wheel in anger. Whatever chance he'd had of catching the gunman was gone now.

When he looked up he saw the gunman's rifle lying abandoned on the runway. He turned his attention toward the jungle and saw the gunman, still heading toward it but at a much slower pace. He was limping badly now.

Maybe the cart had hit him when it went out of control, Joe guessed. He grinned and broke into a sprint but didn't get very far. Something slammed into his legs from behind, and down he went on the runway.

He lay there for a second, stunned. Finally he felt someone plop down heavily on top of him.

Then he heard what sounded like very angry Spanish words.

Joe rolled onto his back and found himself staring up into the face of the driver whose cart he'd stolen.

"Get off me!" Joe shouted. He twisted his head and watched as the gunman climbed the fence and disappeared into the jungle. "He's getting away!"

Eduardo just kept shouting at him, trying to hold him down. Finally Joe managed to throw him off and get to his feet.

Beyond the fence there was no sign of the gunman.

Joe sat down hard on the runway and glared up at the driver.

"Thanks a lot, Ed," he said.

By the time he walked back to the airplane, Eduardo a few paces behind him, there were police vehicles and ambulances everywhere. Frank was talking to one officer as Joe stepped up.

"Where'd you go?" Frank asked. "And what happened to you?"

"Huh?" Joe looked down at his torn shirt and the dark scrapes on the knees of his khakis.

"I was chasing the gunman," he said, "but he got away." He nodded toward the ambulance. "How's the professor?"

"I don't know," Frank replied. "They took him to the hospital in town a few minutes ago.

That ambulance is a second one they dispatched in case it was needed." He studied his brother again. "You sure *you* don't need it?"

Meanwhile, Eduardo was wagging a finger in the police officer's face and pointing at Joe. The officer finally managed to quiet him down. He put an arm around Eduardo's shoulder to direct him back toward the main terminal. Glaring at Joe, the man departed.

"I want to make a report," Joe said, turning to the officer. "I saw the gunman."

"No entiendo, señor," the officer said, holding up a hand. *"Un momento, por favor."*

"He wants you to wait a minute," Frank translated. He understood a little bit of Spanish. "Probably for an officer who speaks English."

Frank watched as another police car drove up, lights flashing. A short, heavyset man with a thick mustache climbed out and surveyed the area. "Must be the boss," Frank said to Joe.

His brother nodded as the newcomer walked over to join them.

"I am Lieutenant Diego Hoyil," the man announced, his English perfect. "And you are—"

"Frank and Joe Hardy."

"I got a good look at the gunman, Lieutenant," Joe began. "I'm sure I could recognize him again."

"You flew in with Professor Ortega," Hoyil interrupted. It was more of a statement than a question, but Joe answered, anyway.

53

"That's right."

The lieutenant motioned two officers forward and indicated that they should flank the Hardys.

"Come with me, please," Hoyil announced.

"Why?" Frank asked, acting innocent. He knew what the problem had to be.

"I want to speak with you. So you will come with me." The lieutenant looked angry, as if he wasn't used to explaining anything to anyone.

"If it's all the same to you, sir," Frank began, "we'd like to go to the hospital first, to make sure the professor is all right."

"If necessary, I am prepared to arrest you," Hoyil said.

"Now, wait a minute," Joe said angrily. Maybe Ortega was right about the Mexican police after all. "We're not crooks. I just got shot at back there. You can't tell me that's against the law here."

"Getting shot at is no crime," the lieutenant agreed. "However, consorting with known thieves is."

"What?" Joe asked.

"Your friend, Professor Ortega," Hoyil replied, opening the back door of his squad car for them. "He is a suspected smuggler accused of stealing our country's national treasures."

Joe stood there speechless. Frank had guessed right and wasn't surprised.

"Now get in," Hoyil demanded, "or I'll simply put you back on the next plane to America."

Chapter

7

FRANK WAS READY to clamp a hand over Joe's mouth if his brother started to say anything to upset Hoyil further. Frank knew that getting back on the plane wouldn't help Ortega.

"We'll be more than happy to cooperate with you, Lieutenant," Frank said, climbing into the squad car. "Lead the way."

Joe stared at Frank for a minute before climbing in after him. Hoyil got in, and they drove around the back of the main terminal, past a hangar with dozens of smaller aircraft. Frank frowned as they drove by.

"Why are so many of the signs in English here?" he asked.

"A lot of wealthy Americans have private homes here," Hoyil said. "They fly down in their private planes.'' From the tone of his voice it was hard to tell whether that bothered him or not.

"The gunman went into the jungle right there, Lieutenant," Joe said, pointing toward a section of the fence bordering the airport. "Are there roads back there, or—"

"Please," Hoyil interrupted. "I would prefer to wait until we reach the station before we discuss anything."

His brother sank back in his seat, surprised. Frank shrugged. If that's the way Hoyil wanted to play it, he'd just sit back and enjoy the ride.

They pulled out of the airport and onto a highway, following signs directing them north to Cancún. On the right, as they drove, they passed mile after mile of resort hotels and luxurious-looking private homes. Occasionally Frank could see clear through to the beach and the ocean beyond. At his left, though, there was only jungle.

Only twenty years earlier, this whole part of the country had been jungle, Ortega had told him. The Mexican government had studied the entire country before picking Cancún as the site for a new resort.

The highway swung through the center of town and became a wide avenue. Frank caught a glimpse of a series of stucco buildings filled with American-style stores lining either side of the road. They soon turned off onto a side street and stopped in front of a nondescript two-story building. A sign in front said Policía.

Frank and Joe followed Hoyil through a side door and into a featureless cinder-block room with two metal chairs and a long wooden table. Hoyil motioned for Frank and Joe to sit.

"Tell me," he began, "why did you come here with Professor Ortega?"

"Because of my girlfriend," Frank said. He had decided to be selective with the truth. He decided not to mention Richards or the Treasury Department just yet. "She's a student of his back in the States. She couldn't believe he stole anything, so we volunteered to come with the professor to try to help discover the truth."

"The truth is he's guilty," Hoyil said. "Over half the pieces from the dig are missing."

Frank remained silent. That was proof all right, proof that something had been stolen. Not proof of who had done it.

Hoyil leaned back against the table. "Did Ortega mention any people he planned to contact?"

Frank shook his head. "He said he had friends in Cancún, but he never told us who."

Hoyil nodded and began pacing across the room. "Why is that, do you think? Didn't he trust you?"

"He trusted us," Joe said a little defensively. "I'm sure he would have told us once we were settled here."

57

Frank decided to change gears. "Who do you think shot him?"

"One of his partners, perhaps," Hoyil said. "Ortega may have been returning here to ask for more money or to pick up more of his artifacts. I don't know. We'll find out when we get a chance to question him."

"Lieutenant," Joe volunteered, "I saw the gunman."

"I know you did," Hoyil replied. "So did the driver of the luggage cart you encountered. We have his description." The lieutenant shook his head and stopped pacing. "You're a very brave young man, Joe. And a very lucky one. You could have been seriously hurt.

"I hope you two realize just how serious this matter is. Whoever tried to kill Professor Ortega probably knows you were with him and may even believe you're working with him. That could be very dangerous for you, and very bad for me."

Frank understood. "The last thing you need is for two American tourists to wind up hurt or dead."

"Exactly." For the first time Hoyil smiled. "I'm glad you understand. So I know," he said, "that you won't become involved in what is really police business while you're here. You're tourists, so spend your time enjoying yourselves."

The smile disappeared from his face now. "Because if I hear of one instance of your trying to do my job, I will have you thrown out of the country. Immediately. Do I make myself clear?''

Frank couldn't think of anything to say but yes.

"Good," Hoyil said. He opened the door and held it for them. "Which hotel are you staying at?" he asked. "I'll have the airline send your luggage over."

"The Plaza del Sol," Frank replied. Ortega had chosen it for them the night before.

"An excellent choice" Hoyil said. "And it's just around the corner from here. Two streets up, two over."

"Thanks," Frank said. "Lieutenant, could we use your phone to call the hospital before we go? I'd like to find out how the professor is doing."

"I left instructions for my men to notify me as soon as there's any news," Hoyil said. "The wound was not life-threatening. I'm sure he'll be fine."

He led them out to the street. "Have a nice vacation. And I hope I don't see you again, for your own sakes."

Frank waited till they were a block away before he spoke.

"What do you make of that guy?"

"Creepy," Joe said. "And not what I expected."

Frank agreed. "Not from what the professor told us about the local police," he said. Hoyil struck him as anything but incompetent.

"Here's the thing that's bothering me," Joe said. "Who knew Ortega was coming? I mean, someone shot him the second he got off the plane."

Frank ticked off the list of names in his mind. Callie. Dad. Richards at the Treasury Department. He frowned. "The Mexican government may get a list of passengers from the airlines, and some alert official might have remembered who he was." Frank thought they'd be better off tackling the question of motive. Who'd want to shoot Ortega?

And that, unfortunately, was something he could not answer.

As they walked through Cancún Frank was surprised at how much it looked like a typical American beach town. There were a lot of restaurants and souvenir shops. Instead of fast-food hamburgers there were taco stands, and the cars people drove were smaller, but almost everything was familiar.

"There it is," Joe said, pointing. "The Plaza del Sol."

Frank liked their hotel immediately. It wasn't too fancy. It turned out to be a three-story white stone structure with small, clean rooms, an attentive staff, and an outdoor pool. After he and Joe checked in they called the hospital. There was still no word on the professor, so they decided to get something to eat.

Across the street from the hotel was a restaurant with strolling guitarists singing Mexican-sounding songs. A lot of expensively dressed tourists were sitting at the bar, drinking exotic-looking beverages with little pieces of fruit in them.

The maître d' told them there would be an hour's wait for dinner.

"Forget that," Joe said as they walked out. "How about over there?" He pointed up the road.

Frank saw a neon sign on top of a small square building that read Harry's Video Taco.

"You've got to be kidding," he said. "You want to go there?"

"Wait a minute," Joe said. "Look at the fine print on that sign. They've got cable TV!"

Frank groaned as Joe practically broke into a trot. Sometimes he really hated traveling with his brother.

As they got closer to the restaurant, though, he began to smell something delicious. A rack of lamb was grilling on a spit in front of the restaurant. A pineapple, skewered at the top of the spit, dripped its sweet juices down over the lamb, basting it.

"Welcome," the man tending the lamb said, smiling at them.

"Thanks," Frank said. He followed Joe inside but stopped dead at the doorway. There were no customers.

Before he could grab Joe and leave gracefully, a man stepped out from behind the bar and approached them. "Welcome," he said. "Can I get you something to drink?"

"Two colas," Joe said, pulling on Frank's arm and sitting him down at the nearest table.

"I'll be back in a minute to take your orders," the waiter said. "This is the best Mexican restaurant in Cancún."

Frank raised an eyebrow. Sure it was, he thought. He barely glanced at the menu, having decided that he'd eat a little something here to keep Joe company, then get his dinner later. After all, he was starving. The food on the airplane had been inedible.

Harry's turned out to be a great restaurant. Joe ordered something called chicken tinga. It smelled so good that Frank insisted on tasting it as soon as it arrived. Tinga was a smoky barbecue-style sauce with some added flavor neither of them could identify. It was the best Mexican food Frank had ever had.

But then his dinner came. He'd ordered chicken as well, served with a chocolate sauce called mole. He asked for seconds as soon as he'd finished, but the waiter talked him into getting something called tacos al pastor instead. That turned out to be the lamb he'd seen sizzling up front, served with pineapple and hot sauce on a little taco shell. There were two shells to an order. He had three orders.

Joe had four.

"Come back tomorrow," the waiter called after them as they left.

"I can't believe it," Frank said after they'd paid the check. He felt as if he were waddling. "I've never eaten that much in my life."

Back at the hotel they called the hospital again and connected with a doctor.

He didn't have good news. Ortega had taken a turn for the worse and was in intensive care. Visiting hours started at ten A.M.

The next morning they were at the hospital at ten sharp. The doctor who had spoken to Frank was still on duty, and he met them at the reception desk.

"There was a lot of bleeding," he said, "but I think we've got it under control now."

"Can we see him?" Frank asked.

The doctor thought a moment. "He'll probably be sleeping, but yes, I suppose so. Only one of you at a time, though."

"You go first," Joe told Frank, who nodded and followed the doctor down the corridor.

Joe turned back to the reception desk to see the nurse behind it smiling at him and pointing down the corridor in the opposite direction.

Joe shrugged. She continued to smile and point. Joe followed her finger to a door that had been propped open at the end of the hall.

"You want me to go there?" he asked. It was

63

probably a waiting area, he thought. He smiled at her and walked down the hall.

Only two very pretty girls were seated in the waiting room. Joe went in and took an empty chair.

"Hi," he said.

"Hi." A dark-haired girl smiled at Joe. The blond one glanced up but immediately went back to reading her magazine.

It was the issue of *Auto & Driver* with Conrado's Tucker on the front.

"Wow. You like cars?" Joe blurted out.

The blond girl stared at him and shook her head. "It's my friend's magazine."

Boyfriend, probably, he thought glumly, though he kept the smile glued to his face.

"That's a nice car on the cover," he offered.

"Yeah, it is," the dark-haired girl spoke up. "My name's Maren Vegard. Miss Friendly over there is Yvette Ducharme."

"Joe Hardy," he said, leaning over to shake hands. He smiled at Yvette, who just kept reading her magazine.

"What brings you here?" he asked Maren.

"A friend of ours fell off a horse last night and hurt his leg," Maren said, brushing her long, dark hair out of her eyes. Joe had the feeling he'd seen her before somewhere. "What about you?"

"Just visiting an old friend who, uh, got sick. Are you in Mexico long?" he asked.

"I'm not sure how long we'll be staying," Maren said. She kept playing with her hair. "Our photo shoot was scheduled for the next couple of days, but now . . ."

That was why she looked so familiar. "You're a model. You do jeans commercials."

"That's right," Maren said.

"I'm a model, too," Yvette said without raising her eyes. "But I don't do jeans."

"That's because they didn't ask you," Maren said.

"So what happened to your shoot?" Joe asked.

"Our photographer's assistant is the one who hurt his leg. Without him, I'm not sure what we'll do," she said.

"Here they are at last," Yvette said, standing. "Steven! Ronnie!"

Joe turned to the doorway. His eyes widened. Ronnie was the tall girl he'd met on the plane, and she was glaring at him even now.

The man with her, the friend who'd supposedly injured himself horseback riding, was the gunman who had tried to kill Professor Ortega!

JOE COULDN'T THINK of a thing to say, but Ronnie solved that problem for him.

"It's the geek from the plane," she said. "What are you doing here?"

Joe glared right back at her. "I wasn't looking for you."

"You two know each other?" Maren asked.

Ronnie snorted. "Barely. And not by choice."

Yvette walked over to Steven and took his arm. "Are you okay, Steven?"

"Better than okay, darling," the man said, smiling. Steven was in his mid-twenties, had short, dark hair, and was wearing an expensive-looking green shirt.

He might be a fashion photographer, but he was also the gunman. Joe was sure of it. He just hoped Steven hadn't recognized him.

"The doctor says it's just a sprain," Steven said, patting Yvette's hand. "I should be able to throw these crutches away in a couple of days."

"That's wonderful!" Yvette said, smiling. "Now, why don't we get out of this horrid place?"

"Wait a minute, Yvette. Where are your manners?" He was staring directly at Joe. "Aren't you going to introduce me to your friend?"

Just then Frank walked into the waiting room. His brother was with three incredibly beautiful girls. Frank almost laughed.

Then he saw the expression on his brother's face. Something was wrong.

"I'm Frank Hardy," he said, stepping forward and introducing himself to each of the strangers in turn. "And I guess you know my brother, Joe."

"I don't," the man on the crutches said. "Steven Santos." He extended his hand, and Joe shook it. The strange expression Frank had seen on his brother's face was gone now, but there was still something wrong.

"Why are you making friends with these guys?" one of the girls asked.

"Oh, take it easy, Ronnie." Maren stood and smiled. "Don't be so stuck-up."

"I'm not stuck-up!" Ronnie exclaimed. She pointed a finger at Joe. "He called me Madonna!"

Maren and Yvette tried to stifle their giggles but failed.

"It's not the first time that's happened," Maren said. "You do have an attitude sometimes, Ronnie."

"I do not!" she said, frowning, which only sent her two friends into more fits of laughing.

Frank would've laughed, too, but he was too concerned about his brother.

"It was nice meeting you, but we have to get going now," Frank announced.

"Wait," Maren said, turning to Santos. "Let's invite them to the party."

The young man smiled. "That's a very good idea," he said. Balancing on his crutches, he reached into his back pocket and pulled out his wallet. He took out a business card, which he handed to Frank.

"We're having a small get-together tonight at eight o'clock, at the address on the card," he said. "Please try to make it."

"We'll try," Frank said.

He led Joe out of the hospital and down the street. A block away, they found a bench, where they sat down. Frank listened to his brother's story.

"Hoyil's never going to take your word that Santos is the gunman," he said when Joe had finished. "Why would a photographer's assistant try to kill Ortega?"

"Maybe we can find out more about him at

the party tonight," Joe said. "Then we can tell Hoyil about him."

Frank nodded. "Do you think Santos recognized you?"

"I couldn't tell. If he did—"

"Then we'd better be very careful around him," Frank said, finishing his sentence. "He doesn't seem to have any problem with shooting people he doesn't like."

"Hey, that's right," Joe said. "I almost forgot to ask. How was the professor?"

"He looks all right. They expect him to wake up some time tonight or maybe tomorrow."

"Good," Joe said. "So what'll we do next?"

Frank considered the options a moment. Without any contacts, and without Ortega to talk to, they didn't have a lot to go on.

"I can think of two things," he said. "One, we can try to contact the Mexican authorities who were in charge at Cobá. They might talk to us about the dig. Or we could do a little exploring on our own. Check out some of the antique shops here, try to find out more about the black market Ortega was talking about."

Joe smiled. "I haven't had good experiences with the authorities here. I vote for number two."

"All right." Frank nodded and stood. "Let's get started."

They learned that most of the antiques stores in Cancún were scattered off the town's main square, just next to the road leading out to the peninsula resorts. The first three stores they went into were run by displaced Americans, and they were more like tacky souvenir stands than antiques shops.

The fourth store was located down an alleyway, farther back from the road than the others had been. As Frank swung the door open a small bell rang, announcing their presence.

This place didn't have a ton of cheap souvenirs. In fact, it was almost empty. Most of an entire wall was taken up by a huge display case filled with earrings, which a sign proudly announced were handmade. A jewelry case next to the cash register was filled with various gold and silver trinkets that could actually have been antiques. The remaining space in the store was taken up by plain wooden shelving, which was covered with native pottery.

Frank was checking out some of the jewelry when he heard the shop owner emerge from behind him.

"Cómo le parecen estos pendientes?"

He turned to find a girl about his age standing behind the cash register. She had on a simple blue and white dress, and her dark hair was pulled back with a barrette.

"Habla inglés?" Frank asked the girl if she spoke English.

"You bet," she said. "Baltimore, Maryland. Born and bred."

"Great," Frank said, smiling broadly and stepping forward. "My brother and I"—he indicated Joe—"are in the market for some native artifacts."

She smiled. "Everything you see in here is one hundred percent native. We don't stock any of that machine-produced stuff."

Frank nodded. "These pieces are all very nice," he said. "But we were looking for something a little older. You know, Mayan jade or something. Some jewelry, maybe."

"Sorry." The girl shook her head. "It doesn't come any older than this. Not legally."

"I know that," Frank said quietly. "But there are ways of getting those things, aren't there?"

"As I said," the girl told him, "that's all illegal. And dangerous."

Frank shrugged. "I don't mind living dangerously."

The girl's face changed immediately. "I think you'd better leave. We don't want any of your business."

"Is there a problem here, Sara?" A man stepped through the curtain behind the cash register. He was thin, with gray hair and wire-rimmed glasses, and spoke in a sharp, clipped voice.

"They're looking for black-market stuff, Dad," the girl said.

"Really?" The man suddenly became as upset

71

as his daughter. "College boys out to make a fast buck off the natives, is that it?"

"No," Frank began. "I've given you the wrong impression."

"Oh, I know exactly what you meant," the man said. "Carlos? Antonio?"

Two heavyset men in work clothes suddenly appeared behind him, filling the doorway. One of them had a crowbar in his hand.

"So much for finding things out on our own," Joe whispered, coming up behind him. "Let's get out of here."

"Right," Frank said. They could save the explanations for another day.

"We're going now," he said, and began slowly backing away.

"Carlos! Antonio!" her father shouted. "Stop them!" Frank realized the shopkeeper didn't want them to leave. The two men quickly moved out from behind the counter and blocked the door.

"Don't go just yet," the shopkeeper said. "I know someone who'll have a lot of questions for you."

Chapter

9

THE MAN with the crowbar lifted it to fling at Joe! This had suddenly gotten serious.

Thinking quickly, Joe spun and kicked the crowbar out of the man's hand. It went flying backward, and a whole shelf of pottery crashed to the floor.

Joe turned and saw the shopkeeper reach beneath the cash register and come up with a gun. Frank charged the man, chopping down hard on his wrist and following with a right cross to his jaw.

Joe was now being attacked by the second man, whom he slam-kicked, sending the man flying backward.

Frank turned away from the older man on the floor, and his eyes widened.

"Joe! Look out!"

Joe heard a whooshing sound in the air and ducked just in time to avoid being flattened by the crowbar, which whistled past his ear.

Both Carlos and Antonio were back on their feet, and they both looked angry.

Frank and one of them circled each other warily, hands raised. The other had recovered his balance after his first wild swing and was now coming at Joe with the crowbar again. Joe ducked to the side, intending to come up beneath the man's swing and flip him over.

He didn't quite make it.

As he drove his shoulder into the man's chest, the end of the crowbar caught him square in the back. He'd never been hit so hard in his life. The momentum of his charge was all that kept him from falling to the ground. It was strong enough to send his attacker crashing into the display case of earrings. The glass window protecting the earrings shattered into a million pieces.

"Stop it!" the girl yelled. "You're wrecking the store!"

Both Joe and his attacker crashed heavily to the floor. Joe's eyes stayed open. The other man's didn't.

Joe turned his head and saw Frank standing over the other workman, rubbing the knuckles of his right hand. "I guess that takes care of that," he said. He bent over, put his hands on his knee, and took a deep breath.

"Not quite."

Joe and Frank turned. The shopkeeper's daughter had picked up her father's gun and had it pointed directly at them. She held the pistol as if she knew how to use it. "Get your hands up."

Fifteen minutes later both of them were securely tied to stout wooden chairs in the back room of the shop.

The shopkeeper stood nearby, holding an ice pack to his jaw. Joe had heard him talking on the phone while they were being tied up but was unable to make out what he was saying. His daughter stood next to him. Carlos and Antonio, meanwhile, were leaning up against a heavy wooden table behind the shopkeeper.

He heard the bell at the front door of the shop ring. The girl went to answer it, and a few seconds later she returned with a tall, gray-haired woman.

"What happened to you?" the newcomer asked, looking at the shopkeeper.

"We had a little . . . altercation," he said, rubbing his jaw.

"I can see that." The woman turned and examined Frank and Joe. "They look kind of young to be smugglers, George."

"We're not smugglers," Joe said.

"What do you want with illegal artifacts, then?" the shopkeeper asked.

"George, please. Let me ask the questions. My name is Luz Montoya," she said. "I'm with the Department of Antiquities. And you are—"

"Frank Hardy. And this is my brother, Joe."

She pulled up a chair. "Let me tell you boys something. Walking into an antiques store and asking questions about illegal artifacts is not the way to make a good impression here. Sentiments run high in Mexico, especially where our national treasures are concerned. The country was looted wholesale in the nineteenth century by foreigners, and people here won't stand for it anymore—especially after last summer."

"The dig at Cobá," Joe said.

Montoya's eyebrows rose. "You know about that?"

Joe started to answer, but his brother interrupted him.

"If you don't mind, could you show us some identification?" Frank asked.

The woman shrugged and held out a plastic ID card for them to examine. It appeared to be genuine.

"Thank you," Frank said. And then he told her the whole story of how they'd come to be in Cancún. When he got to the part about Ortega being shot the woman's mouth dropped open in surprise.

"What? Is Rafael all right?"

"He's out of danger." Frank nodded. "The

doctors say he should be up and talking by tomorrow."

"Thank goodness for that, at least," Montoya said. "He's a good friend. We both worked for the Smithsonian when we got out of college in the States."

Something clicked in Joe's head.

"You're the one who told him about Xavier Antiques."

"That's right," she said. She smiled at Joe as if she'd made a decision, then turned back to the shopkeeper. "George, why don't you untie these boys? I think we owe them an apology."

"I agree," the shopkeeper said, bending down to loosen their bonds. "I'm George Archer, and this is my daughter, Sara. Those two men are Antonio and Carlos Gutierrez."

"So you don't believe the accusations against the professor either?" Frank asked.

Montoya sighed. "No, I don't."

"You're too trusting, Luz," Archer said. "He was in the perfect spot to make a little easy money."

"You're too cynical," she shot back. "Who's the officer handling his shooting?"

"A man named Lieutenant Hoyil," Joe said.

Archer made a face.

"He's not so bad, George," Montoya said. "You know how many of the black marketeers he's caught over the last few months."

The shopkeeper snorted. "I wouldn't be surprised if he's just eliminating the competition."

"I know that you and the lieutenant have had your differences in the past," Montoya said. "But we're all going to work together now to try to eliminate smuggling, aren't we?"

"I'll work with you, thanks," Archer said. "Not him."

She laughed. "Well," she said, standing, "I'm glad this turned out to be just a misunderstanding. I have enough to do right now as it is. Frank and Joe, it was nice to meet you. George, Sara—"

"Could we come by and talk to you tomorrow?" Frank interrupted.

The woman nodded. "Of course. The department has an office on the main square. I should be there all day."

With those words she left. Frank and Joe followed a few minutes later.

"I noticed you didn't mention Santos," Joe said as they started walking back to their hotel. "Didn't you trust her?"

"More than Hoyil," Frank said. "But I thought it would be worth making a phone call to Richards to check out both of them when we get back to the hotel."

Joe stopped suddenly, recognizing where they were.

Right in front of Harry's Video Taco.

The same man was out front, cooking lamb that smelled as good as it had the night before.

"Hello." Their waiter stood at the front door, waving to them.

"I hear the dinner bell, Frank," Joe said. "Come on."

"Dinner?" Frank looked at his watch. "It's three o'clock."

"Don't listen to the clock. Listen to that," Joe said, pointing to the lamb. "What is it telling you?"

Frank smiled. "Tacos al pastor time?"

"Exactly," Joe said. "Tacos al pastor time."

By the time they finished eating and got back to the hotel, Joe felt so full that all he wanted to do was lie down. But when he opened the door to their room someone was on his bed already.

Lieutenant Hoyil. And two other police officers.

"I hope you've enjoyed your sightseeing. I have something else you might be interested in looking at," Hoyil continued.

The lieutenant tossed a small cloth bag held tight with a drawstring to Joe.

Joe reached into the bag and pulled out a huge piece of jade. There were carvings all along one side of it.

"Cloud Ixmix," Frank said, examining the hieroglyphs. "It's the same seal as the one on Mrs. Conrado's medallion."

"We found that piece early this afternoon, in the house Ortega rented last summer," Hoyil said. "Hidden beneath one of the floorboards."

He took the jade back from Frank and handed it to one of his officers. "As soon as your Professor Ortega is released from the hospital he'll be arrested and charged with smuggling.

"And then"—the lieutenant smiled—"we will lock him up. For a long, long time."

Chapter

10

JOE COULDN'T believe it. "Could someone else have lived in that house?" he asked.

The lieutenant's expression darkened. Clearly he wasn't used to having his word questioned. "The man who rented the house to Ortega hasn't set foot in it since last summer, nor has any other tenant."

"Any progress on finding the gunman?" Frank asked.

Hoyil's expression darkened still further. "I'm afraid not," he said. "But I suspect that once Ortega is confronted with this evidence, the entire case will become clearer." He stepped past them into the corridor. "I thought you'd want to know about this." He smiled. "Enjoy the rest of your stay here."

Frank shut the door after him and the two officers. "He seemed to have fun doing that."

"Do you think he's even trying to find the gunman?" Joe asked. "He seems a lot more concerned about nailing the professor."

"I noticed," Frank said. "I think we should take Ortega's accusations about the police around here very seriously."

Joe nodded. "Except that Montoya said Hoyil was all right. It could be that someone's feeding him false information about Ortega."

"The real smugglers," Frank said, yawning. He tried to get Richards on the phone but could only leave a message. Then he flopped down on his bed and closed his eyes. "I need a nap before we go to that party tonight."

"You don't think we need to get dressed up for it, do you? The most formal piece of clothing I've got is a Hawaiian shirt."

"I packed for Florida, too," his brother said. "We're going to look like twins."

Joe groaned. He could see it now. That Ronnie girl was going to be making fun of him all night long.

After resting, Frank and Joe put on their Hawaiian shirts and phoned for a taxi. It was a little after eight o'clock by the time they arrived at the party. It was in one of the mansions right on the beach just north of the airport.

The place was wall-to-wall people. Most of the

men were in tuxedos. Most of the women were in expensive gowns, except for the younger women.

In one corner of the room he saw Yvette. She acknowledged his presence with a slight nod of her head, which was now covered with long black hair.

"Wait a minute," Frank said. "Wasn't she a blonde this morning?"

Joe nodded.

"Joe! Frank!"

They turned and saw Maren making her way through the crowd toward them. She was a blonde now.

"This modeling business is pretty confusing," Frank said.

"Come on," Maren said, taking each of them by one hand. "There are some people you have to meet."

All the guests seemed pleasant enough, but Joe soon lost track of their names. From the dazed expression on his brother's face he could tell Frank wasn't having much better luck.

After about ten minutes Joe had had enough.

He wandered out onto a terrace overlooking the beach.

A woman—older, probably, judging from the expensive-looking gown she was wearing—was standing at the rail overlooking the ocean, her back to him. A couple was conversing quietly at the far end of the terrace.

Other than these three, Joe was alone. He felt himself begin to unwind.

This was more like it, he thought. He stared up at a sky full of stars and tried to pick out a few constellations. He soon realized the skies were different here.

He turned back to look at the house. Small terraces like the one he was standing on jutted out from the floor above him as well. There were expensive-looking statues perched on the corners of each one. To his right was a set of stairs leading down to the beach and a private boat house.

The woman at the railing turned, and he was startled. It was Ronnie.

His eyes widened. If he thought she looked good before—

"What are you staring at now?" she demanded, planting her hands on her hips.

"I wasn't staring!" Joe said hotly. "I just thought you were somebody else, that's all!"

"Yeah? Like who?" Ronnie glared at him.

"It's not important." Joe exhaled a breath he hadn't even realized he was holding. "Look, I just came out here to get a little air. I didn't mean to disturb you."

"You didn't disturb me," she said, brushing past him. "And I'll leave you to your air."

"Wait," Joe blurted out. Ronnie stopped in midstride, one foot on the terrace, the other on the carpeted floor of the main house, and turned back to face him.

"Well?"

"I just wanted to say I was sorry. For backing into you on the plane," Joe began. "That kind of got us off on the wrong foot." He looked at her again and shrugged.

She studied him for a moment, then turned and stepped back onto the terrace.

"Well, I'm sorry, too. I shouldn't have called you a geek."

"Forget it. I was kind of out of it that day anyway."

"I noticed," she said. "Any particular reason why?"

Joe shook his head. "Let's talk about something else," he said. The two of them were standing at the railing now, looking out over the ocean. "Like why you aren't back there in the party, meeting all those important people."

"Not for me." She shook her head. "I can take about ten minutes of it, no more." She leaned on the railing with one elbow and turned to face him. "How long did you last?"

"About ten minutes," Joe admitted, laughing. The wind picked up for a second, carrying the smell of the ocean up from the beach below and blowing a stray lock of hair into Ronnie's face. She brushed it back.

"I'm getting the impression modeling isn't what you want to spend your life doing."

"You've got that right."

"So if you don't want to be a model, what is it you want to do?"

She turned away, leaning forward over the railing again. "As you said, let's talk about something else."

"Come on," Joe pressed.

"You'd laugh if I told you."

"No, I wouldn't."

Ronnie stared back out over the ocean. "Well," she said quietly, her eyes not leaving the horizon, "I want to be a race car driver."

Joe couldn't help it. He laughed.

"I knew it." Ronnie pushed herself back from the railing and stomped off toward the house. "I knew it, I knew it, I knew it—"

"No, wait," Joe said. He grabbed Ronnie's arm and held on to it as she tried to twist free. "I think that's what I might want to do someday, too. If I can't be a detective, that is."

He stopped talking as he realized Ronnie was the one laughing now.

"What's so funny?"

"I can't picture you as a detective. At least, not in that shirt."

He pretended to be hurt. "What's wrong with this shirt?"

"Not a thing, actually. You can let go of me now, you know," she said.

"I know," Joe said. He loosened his grip a little but didn't let go.

It was very quiet all of a sudden, and Joe could hear someone moving around on the terrace above them.

"I don't feel like going back to the party," Ronnie said.

Joe nodded. "Me, neither. How about a walk on the beach?"

"You read my mind." She slipped her hand into his.

Joe felt something drift against his hair. He reached up and pulled away a few flakes of something soft and white that crumbled in his hand. Plaster dust.

"What's the matter?" Ronnie asked.

Joe shook his head and raised his eyes.

"Move, Ronnie!" he shouted.

One of the statues on the terrace above them was wobbling, and suddenly it was hurtling straight down toward them!

Chapter

11

"WHERE DID your brother go?" Maren asked. Frank had no idea. Joe had given them the slip.

He finally did have a chance to ask Maren some questions now, though. "I'm sure he'll turn up. But what about your friend Steven? Where is he?"

"Around," she said. "You can usually find him and Yvette cuddling in some corner. Although with this many people in the house, they probably went off somewhere to hide. Which means you'll never find them. Steven knows every room in this house."

Frank was about to ask what she meant by that when he felt someone tap him on the shoulder. He turned and found himself face-to-face with Sara Archer.

"Sara! What are you doing here?"

"I could ask you the same thing," she said. She was wearing a green-and-red dress and had her hair pulled back from her face. The style made her look five years older.

"Joe and I met Maren at the hospital earlier today," he said. "Do you two know each other?" He began to introduce Maren, but she had taken off.

"Well, that's her," he said, pointing to where she was talking with two men.

"She's one of the models, isn't she? For Faces International?" she asked excitedly. "You've got to introduce me. I'm trying to sell them on using some of my jewelry for their shoot. It'll be a big break if I can get it."

Frank frowned. "How'd you get an invitation if you don't know anybody? This seems like a pretty exclusive party."

"My dad knows the agency's owner pretty well. The guy's a big customer at our shop." She pointed out a handful of colorfully glazed pots that decorated a nearby bookshelf. "He bought a whole crateful of those last month," she said. "Hey! There's Thome!" She pointed to a tall, white-haired man who had suddenly become the center of attention a few feet from them. She pronounced his name "tom-ay."

"Thome?"

"Thome. The photographer," she said. "Don't tell me you don't know who he is."

"No," Frank admitted. "Does he have a last name?"

"He doesn't need a last name," Sara said. "He's the world's most famous photographer."

In whose opinion? Frank was about to ask when he heard a loud crash, followed by a woman's scream. Both sounded as if they came from outside the house.

"What was that?" Sara asked.

"I don't know," Frank replied, taking her by the arm. "Let's find out."

Frank made his way out to the terrace and was surprised to see a shaken Ronnie holding on to his brother.

"What happened?" Frank asked.

"That fell," Joe said, pointing at the statue, which had shattered into a thousand pieces on the terrace. "From up there."

Joe knew Frank was asking himself the exact same questions that he was.

Was it an accident? Or was it Santos?

"Veronica?" Frank turned and saw Thome rushing out onto the terrace. "Are you all right?"

"I'm fine now," Ronnie said. "These are my friends, Frank and Joe Hardy. Joe, Frank, this is Thome, our photographer."

"Pleased to meet you," Frank said.

"Joe just saved my life." Ronnie took his arm again and smiled.

The white-haired man inclined his head ever

so slightly and peered at Joe from behind his sunglasses.

"I am forever in your debt, young man."

"What happened?" Santos, with Yvette hanging on to his arm, was walking toward them. His crutches were gone, and he was using a cane. He was more than healthy enough to have pushed the statue over, the Hardys observed.

"An accident," Thome said. "Though thanks to our new friend here"—he put an arm around Joe's shoulder—"Veronica was not injured."

Santos looked down at the remnants of the statue, then up at Ronnie and Joe. "How fortunate," he said.

"Our shoot seems to be jinxed, Steven." Thome removed his sunglasses and rubbed his eyes. "First your injury, and now this. Veronica, will you be able to work tomorrow?"

"I think so," she said.

"We can put the shoot off a day if we need to." Thome put his sunglasses back on. "Steven will only be able to go at half speed tomorrow, anyway. I would have to do a lot of the setup work myself."

"I'll be fine tomorrow," Santos insisted.

Thome raised an eyebrow. "I'm not so sure about that."

"I've got an idea," Ronnie said. "Why don't you ask Joe to help us out?" She turned and smiled at him. "What do you say? It would just be until Steven can get around again."

"No problem," Joe said.

"Impossible," Santos said quickly. "He has no knowledge of the site, no knowledge of what to do on a shoot."

"He won't need it if you're there," Ronnie said. "He can just do what you and Thome tell him to. That way we can stay on schedule."

"I like the idea," Thome said, studying Joe thoughtfully. "Do you know anything about photography?"

"Enough to get by," Joe said. Frank could give him a crash course in some of the basics. This would give him a chance to keep an eye on Santos and maybe find out a little more about the man.

"It's all settled, then," Thome said. "Meet us here at four tomorrow morning."

"Four? In the morning?" Joe gulped.

"So we can catch the early-morning sun," Ronnie said. "It's a two-hour drive there."

"What's this place called again, Steven?" Thome asked. "I never can keep all these Mexican names straight in my mind."

Santos was silent a moment.

"Cobá," he finally said.

"Cobá, exactly. That's it," Thome said.

"Excuse me." Joe turned and found Sara Archer standing at his side. "I just wanted to say hello to Mr. Thome," she said in a much sweeter voice than she had used that afternoon. "I've been a big fan of yours for years."

The photographer smiled at her. "And you are—"

"This is Sara Archer, a friend of ours," Frank said, stepping forward.

"I'm a jewelry designer," she said, taking Thome's hand.

"Those are beautiful earrings you have on," Ronnie said. She let go of Joe's arm and stepped closer to Sara to look at them. "Are they your own design?"

Sara nodded.

"They are beautiful." Thome nodded. "Perhaps we can use some of them on the shoot."

"Frank and Joe know how to get in touch with me." she said.

"Good. And now I think we've all had enough excitement for one night." He clapped his hands for attention. "I'm sorry to disappoint you, but this party is over. Go home, everyone. Go home."

The last thing Joe saw as he left was Santos glaring at him.

"Are you okay?" Frank asked as they headed back toward Cancún in the taxi one of the house staff had called for them.

"Ronnie was the one who had the close call. I'm fine." He looked at his brother. "I find it hard to believe that was an accident."

"So do I," his brother said. "And I find it hard to believe it's just a coincidence that the modeling shoot is happening at Cobá."

"Me, too," said Joe. "You could talk to Montoya tomorrow. Ask her what she knows about it."

Frank nodded. "I will. I've also got about a million other questions for her." He was silent a moment. "You'd better be very careful on that shoot. Don't turn your back on Santos for a minute."

"I'll try not to," Joe said as they pulled up in front of their hotel.

"I think I'm a little too keyed up to sleep yet," Joe said. He looked down the street.

Harry's was still open.

"Say," he said, turning to Frank. "Are you, by any chance, hungry?"

When Joe arrived at the mansion the next morning it seemed as though he had never left. But the party was long over, and everyone was ready for work. Five models, including Ronnie and Yvette, a makeup woman, Santos, and a big bearded man Joe hadn't seen before were all standing next to a large bus, waiting for him. Thome, he was informed, would follow later on his motorcycle, with Maren.

Joe soon discovered that everyone except Ronnie regarded him as an errand boy. He put luggage on the van, bought coffee, retrieved forgotten items from hotel rooms, and so on. When they finally set out on the road for Cobá with the big man, whose name was Vinicio, behind the wheel, he fell right asleep.

The next thing he knew, someone was shaking his shoulder. "Hey, wake up." He cracked one eyelid and found himself staring up at Ronnie. "We're here," she said.

Joe twisted in his seat to gaze out the window. The sky was just beginning to lighten to gray. They'd parked on the side of a small dirt road where two small pigs rooting in the grass next to the bus was being chased by a small girl.

"Hardy!" Santos stood near the driver's seat, glaring at him. "Come. We have work to do. And you, Ronnie, should be in makeup."

"I'll see you later," she told Joe, disappearing into the back of the bus where he could hear the other models preparing for the shoot.

"Bring those bags and follow me," Santos said brusquely, stepping out of the bus. He was still using a cane, but his limp was almost completely gone now. Joe slung the bags Santos had pointed to over his shoulder and stepped outside.

The sun was just peeking through the trees, and it gave the jungle an eerie purplish glow. Joe walked up a small path, stopping at a wooden gate with a little ticket booth next to it. The entrance to the dig, no doubt, he concluded.

Ortega had told them a great deal of Cobá was still unexplored, and Joe could immediately see that that was true. As they passed through the gate Joe noticed a large pyramid that was partly overgrown, directly to his right.

"Put those down here," Santos said as they made their way into a small clearing. "Then I'll need you to prepare the first site."

As Joe set the bags down Santos grabbed the largest one and snapped it open. He pulled out a small, heavy metal case and handed it and a long camera tripod to Joe.

"Go through that grove of trees there," Santos said, pointing off to the right. "You'll find a small group of buildings with a row of steps in front. Clean off the steps and set up the tripod. Take a reading with the light meter in the case. You can come back when everything's ready."

The trail Santos had pointed out to him was easy to follow for the first few hundred feet, but by the time he had been walking for ten minutes Joe knew he was completely lost.

"Hey!" he called out.

The only response was a few bird calls and some other animal noises he didn't recognize. Then unexpectedly, a few hundred feet ahead of him, he saw Santos.

How had he gotten over there?

"This way," Santos called out. "You must've gotten off the trail."

Or you were trying to get rid of me? Joe thought. Somebody could disappear forever in this jungle.

The path beneath his feet was thick with underbrush. One foot got caught on a branch, and he had to shake it free.

Now the trail was gone altogether, and Santos was barely visible through the trees.

"This way, Hardy!"

"Coming, master," Joe grumbled under his breath. He shifted the heavy case of equipment to his right hand and grabbed the tripod with his left. A huge yellow butterfly fluttered across his path, and he brushed it away with the tripod. Sighing, he took another step forward.

Suddenly the ground gave way beneath his feet.

"What the—"

Joe glanced down and caught a glimpse of a gaping open pit below him.

Chapter

12

FRANTICALLY JOE TRIED to regain his balance but couldn't. If he fell into the pit he wouldn't be coming out.

As he slid forward he knew he had only one chance.

He let go of the photography case and grabbed onto the long camera tripod with both hands.

He was falling.

And then he wasn't.

The tripod was just long enough to bridge the mouth of the pit!

He hung in midair, suspended over the pit. Far below he heard the photography equipment crash against something hard. Then there was a distant splashing sound.

Water. This might be a well, possibly even

one of those cenotes he and the professor had talked about. He might have just made a very important archaeological discovery.

Of course, he had to get out of there alive first. He opened his mouth to yell for help, and a nasty thought crossed his mind. Why would the top of the well have been hidden? Unless it was a trap. And he had a pretty good idea of who had set this trap—Santos.

He decided to get out under his own power. He slowly slid along the tripod legs toward the edge of the pit.

After a moment he looked up. Sweat was dripping into his eyes, stinging them, but there was nothing he could do about that now. Suddenly the tripod moved! Loose dirt from the path above fell in his eyes. Joe knew that one more little slide could cause him to fall deep into the cenote.

He had to call for help.

"Hey! Anybody out there, help!"

No response. He held on to the tripod, willing himself not to move. Whether it was one minute or five minutes or even ten minutes later, he couldn't tell. The muscles in his arms were trembling already.

"Joe!"

It was Ronnie.

"Ronnie! Down here!"

Her face appeared at the edge of the pit. Then Maren was there and Yvette and even Santos.

The next few seconds were a blur, but somehow Joe was pulled out of the well and onto solid ground.

"What happened?" Ronnie asked.

Joe shook his head. "I was walking down the trail here when the ground just disappeared from under me."

"I thought this was all supposed to be clearly marked," Ronnie said angrily, turning to Santos.

"It was," he insisted.

Joe frowned. Santos could have moved all the warning signs.

Thome came running down the trail. Maren quickly filled him in on what had happened.

Thome turned to Santos. "It was on your recommendation we came to these ruins, Steven, even though they are unexplored. You assured me they were entirely safe."

Now that was interesting, Joe thought. Doing the shoot here was Santos's idea?

The photographer turned to Joe and shook his head. "I realize that this is not your fault, Joe, but all that equipment is not so easily replaced," he said. "We can work without it, but—"

"I'm sorry, sir," Joe said. "But think of it this way. Can you imagine the look on the face of the archaeologist who discovers that the Maya invented the camera?"

Everyone burst out laughing—everyone, that is, except Santos.

"All right," Thorne said, clapping his hands. "Let's get to work, then."

"Are you all right?" Ronnie asked Joe as the group around the well broke up.

'I'm fine," Joe said. He was watching Santos, who was walking with Yvette. The two of them were laughing.

"Good," Ronnie said. "Hey, I just realized something. You saved my life, and I saved yours. We're even now."

Joe forced a smile. "Let's hope we stay that way."

As he pushed through the hospital doors Frank was trying to decide which question to ask Professor Ortega first.

So much had happened since just the day before yesterday, when the professor had been shot, and a lot of it he still couldn't put together. What was the modeling agency's connection with the smuggling? And what about the smuggling ring? Who else besides Santos was involved in it?

And what would the professor have to say about the new evidence Hoyil had discovered?

"Buenos días," he said to the nurse behind the reception desk, a short, brown-haired woman. "Rafael Ortega, *por favor.*"

"Ortega?" She flipped through a small file of index cards and pointed to a number. Frank saw that the professor was in room 203.

He rode the elevator to the second floor, found room 203, and knocked on the door. There was no response.

Maybe he's sleeping, Frank thought. He pushed the door open and saw only an empty bed in the center of the room.

"Professor?"

He stepped all the way in and shut the door behind him. Frowning, he went to the closet. It was empty. The bathroom door was open. No one was in there, either.

Frank burst out into the hallway, almost colliding with Ortega's doctor.

"Professor Ortega's gone!" Frank exclaimed.

The doctor peeked inside the room.

"The fool. If he moves around too much, his wound will open and start bleeding again." He looked at Frank. "Why would he leave before he's completely well?"

"He's a fool, all right," Frank said. And not just because his wound might start bleeding again. Sneaking out like that indicated that Ortega had something to hide. Frank couldn't help but think that that something had to do with smuggled artifacts. Now Frank had some additional questions for Luz Montoya.

Frank easily found Montoya's office. It was on the second floor of a two-story brick building right in the center of town. He pressed the

buzzer next to the door and stood by the inter-
com, waiting.

"Excuse me."

Frank saw a bearded man in a three-piece suit
moving down the hall toward him.

"If you're looking for Luz, she's not going to
be in today," the man said. "Something came
up."

Frank took a deep breath and exhaled heavily.
It seemed as if this was his day to miss everybody.

"Is there a phone I can use?" he asked. He
wanted to try Richards once more. He felt he
had to let him know the professor had disappeared.

"Sure," the man said. "You can use mine."

Frank followed him down the hall into another
office, trying to figure out how to explain what
had happened to the treasury agent.

There was still no answer at the number Richards had given him.

"It figures," he said, hanging up. "Thanks
anyway."

The man nodded, and Frank stepped out into
the hallway again. His best bet now would be to
head out to the shoot, where he was to meet
Joe.

Then he saw someone fumbling at Montoya's
door. It looked as though the person was trying
to break in.

Immediately Frank thought it might be Ortega,
but the figure was too small. Whoever it was had

on a shapeless brown poncho, with a hood, that covered everything head to toe.

Frank wanted to know why the person was so interested in what Montoya kept in her office.

Moving quietly, Frank slipped up behind the man and snaked an arm around his neck.

"I don't think that's your office," Frank whispered in the intruder's ear. He was shorter and considerably slighter than Frank had expected. "But maybe if you tell me what you're looking for, I can help you find it."

Chapter

13

IT TOOK FRANK about two-tenths of a second to realize he'd made a mistake. He released his grip immediately.

Sara Archer bent over and began coughing.

"Oh, boy, Sara, I'm sorry," Frank said, leaning over her. He had never been so embarrassed.

"I'm so sorry," he repeated. "I thought you were breaking in."

"I wasn't breaking in!" she shouted. She held out a key in her right hand. "I just can't get this thing to work!"

She glared at him and began massaging her neck.

"Here," Frank said. "Let me try."

He took the key from her and inserted it in the lock. The door opened immediately.

"Come on," she said, stepping inside, "before somebody else jumps out and grabs me."

"Where did you get a key, anyway?" he asked.

"From Luz," she said, flipping on the light switch. She went right to a large metal desk at the center of the office and began rummaging around.

"Where is she? What are you looking for?"

"Just a piece of paper," she said. "There." She picked up a long yellow sheet with some writing on it, folded it carefully, and put it in her pocket. "Let's go."

"Wait a minute, Sara. There's something I have to tell you."

She turned to look at him. "What?"

"Ortega's disappeared from the hospital. If you're taking those numbers to Luz, I think you ought to tell her that."

"Oh," she said, peeling off the brown cloak, and folding it over her arm. "Is that all?"

"Is that all? Don't you understand? This means he's working for the smugglers!" Frank was surprised to hear himself practically yelling.

It didn't seem to bother Sara. She turned off the lights and held the door open for Frank.

"Come on," she said. "I've got something to show you."

Confused, Frank followed her out of the office.

* * *

"More suntan lotion, Hardy," Santos commanded, snapping his fingers.

Barely masking a sigh, Joe stepped forward and squeezed oil onto his hands. As he began to apply it to Maren's neck she sat up straight for him.

Maren was lying on a stone step, one of many that led up to the complex of small buildings Joe had noticed earlier. She was wearing a very small bikini and sunglasses.

As Joe applied the lotion Maren lifted the necklace she was wearing out of his way.

"This thing is so heavy," she said, leaning back on the step. "Do I really need it?"

"Today we do," Thome said absently. "But perhaps we can use something else tomorrow. Maybe the Archer girl's jewelry."

Joe finished applying the lotion and stepped back out of the shot again.

"Now." Thome stepped behind the camera again. "Maren, lean forward a little so that—"

"We shouldn't use the Archer girl's jewelry," Santos said forcefully—so forcefully that Thome stepped back from the camera and raised an eyebrow. "With all due respect," the young man added. "It is your decision, of course, but in a matter like this, authenticity is everything. The reproductions we have picked out duplicate—"

"Hand me the macro lens, Steven," Thome said, cutting him off.

Santos reached into a nearby case and pulled out a lens, which he handed to the photographer.

Thorne took one look at it and tossed it back to him. "That's the zoom," he said acidly. "Haven't you learned anything yet?"

Joe stepped up behind Santos and handed Thorne the correct lens. Frank had spent half an hour going over lens types with him the night before.

"Thank you, Joe," the white-haired man said, snapping the new lens on his camera. He turned back to Maren. "Smile."

How had Santos gotten to be Thorne's assistant on the shoot if he couldn't tell the difference between a zoom and a macro? Joe wondered.

"She's a lot better at this than I am."

Joe turned and saw Ronnie watching Maren, who was busy posing for the camera.

"Joe, what really happened back there?" Ronnie asked suddenly.

"Back there?"

Ronnie opened her mouth to say something else, then shut it as Maren stepped up beside them.

"Here. Your turn to suffer," she said, handing Ronnie the necklace she'd been wearing. "Those Mayan women must have had really strong necks."

Joe noticed the necklace for the first time that day. Suddenly he knew exactly what the connection was between the modeling agency, Santos, and the smuggled artifacts. Those so-called replicas were real!

By the time Sara and he arrived at their destination, Frank was glad he hadn't been able to reach Richards after all.

After they'd left Montoya's office she'd picked up her father's car and driven southwest out of Cancún, into the interior of the country. An hour later they turned off the main road onto a small dirt path, which ended at a run-down–looking shack.

First Montoya and then Ortega emerged from the shack.

The professor was very pale, and he looked as if he'd dropped ten pounds in the day and a half since Frank had seen him. Still, he flashed Frank a broad, friendly smile.

Frank grasped his hand firmly and returned the smile. "I'm glad to see you up and about, Professor, though I'm not so sure it was such a good idea to leave the hospital."

"Luz agrees with you, but I managed to talk her into bringing me here, anyway," he said. "I didn't want to give whoever shot me a second chance. Nor did I want to put you or your brother in any further danger." Ortega frowned. "Where *is* your brother?"

"That's a long story," Frank said. "I'm to meet up with him later tonight. Can we go inside? I've got a lot of questions for you."

"And I'd like to know where Sara found you," Luz said, "but first I want that piece of paper. Did you find it?"

Sara nodded and handed Montoya the sheet she'd taken from the office.

"What is it?" Frank asked.

"The number and address of the man who rented me my house last summer," Ortega said. "Hoyil is making wild accusations about finding another piece of jade from the dig there." The professor looked at Frank and smiled. "He's told you about it already."

Frank nodded.

"Well, one of them is lying," Luz said.

"So we're going to talk to Alfredo Acosta, the man I rented from," Ortega said.

Luz took Ortega by his good arm and turned back toward the shack. "Come on inside, everyone."

Sara started after them, stopping when she reached the doorway and realized Frank wasn't following. "Aren't you coming?" she asked.

He shook his head. "In a minute. I want to think."

She nodded and disappeared inside.

Frank was thinking that Hoyil was a very powerful man around there. If he turned against them, they wouldn't have a chance.

Chapter

14

JOE WAS DRYING OFF after a long, hot bath when Frank arrived at the motel they had picked for a rendezvous point. His brother hadn't come alone.

"Professor!" Joe exclaimed.

"Joe, it's good to see you," Ortega said.

Joe listened as Frank told him everything that had happened that day. "Luz and Sara have gone back to Cancún now. And we've got to meet this Acosta in half an hour at the entrance to the Cobá site. What about you?" his brother asked, sitting down on one of the beds. "You find out any more about Santos?"

"He tried to kill me again," Joe said, pulling on a shirt. "Almost dropped me in a bottomless pit. In fact, it might have been one of those cenotes, Professor."

"At the Cobá site?" Ortega's eyes shone with excitement. "Could you find it again?"

"No problem," he said. "But listen to this, Frank—I don't think Santos knows anything about photography."

His brother looked up. "Oh?"

"He didn't know the difference between a macro and a zoom lens."

"So how did he get on the shoot?"

Joe frowned. "I don't know. Thome said he picked the site for them. Maybe he's their location scout."

"Wait a minute." Ortega shook his head. "I'm not following you. Frank, you said this Santos was the man who shot me? And now he's brought a group of models to Cobá, is that it?"

Frank nodded.

"Well, I don't understand. Why? What does all this have to do with smuggling?" the professor asked.

"I was coming to that," Joe replied. "We know that the smugglers were shipping the Cobá artifacts to Xavier Antiques, right? To sell them to private American collectors?"

Frank and the professor nodded.

"Well, that route got shut down, so while the authorities were busy with you they've been looking for other ways to get their artifacts out of the country." Joe nodded. "And I think I found out what they decided today."

He told Frank and the professor about the jewelry replicas.

"Substitute the real pieces for the fakes?" Ortega shook his head. "There's no way that could work on a large scale."

"It doesn't have to," Joe said. "You yourself said how much money a single piece goes for. They don't even need to use exact replicas, either. All they need is fairly authentic-looking costume jewelry on the way in, and no customs official will stop them on the way out."

"The real pieces must be somewhere nearby. We'd better tell Luz about this," Ortega finished.

"That would make sense," Frank said. "That's how Hoyil got the piece he showed us before. The one he said he found in the house you had last summer."

Joe nodded. The way he figured it, Hoyil had to be part of the smuggling ring. Though he supposed someone could have planted that piece for the lieutenant to find.

Ortega nodded. "Joe, do you think others from the modeling agency are involved in the smuggling?"

"No way," Joe said. "The only one smart enough to be involved in something like this is Ronnie. And she's too smart to be involved in something like this." Frank laughed. "I guess I didn't explain that so well," Joe said.

"Who's Ronnie," Ortega asked just as someone knocked on the door.

Joe got up and peered through the peephole.

"This is Ronnie," he said, opening the door. "Ronnie Lane."

She was dressed in jeans and a racing jacket and held a motorcycle helmet in one hand. "Frank. I didn't expect to find you here." She smiled at Joe. "Come on. I borrowed Thorne's motorcycle. If you behave nicely at dinner, maybe I'll even let you drive."

Joe smacked himself on the forehead. In the excitement he had forgotten he and Ronnie had made plans to have dinner together.

"I have to cancel," he said. "I'm really sorry, but something else came up."

She frowned, then caught sight of Professor Ortega.

"Hello," he said, waving to her with his good arm.

"Ronnie, this is a friend of ours, Professor Rafael Ortega."

"Professor." Ronnie nodded, staring at the sling on Ortega's shoulder. "Wait a minute. I'll bet he's the man you were visiting in the hospital, isn't he?" She looked back and forth from Frank to Joe. "This has something to do with Steven, Joe. You can't fool me."

"This doesn't," Joe said. "Honestly."

"But you wouldn't tell me if it did, would you?" She glared at him. "Why can't you tell me what's going on? What are you, some kind of teen spy?''

Joe shook his head. "That's not it, Ronnie. It's too dangerous.''

"Too dangerous? Don't you remember who had a statue fall on her? Who helped save your life?'' She folded her arms across her chest. "Look, Joe, I'm not stupid. These accidents the last two days haven't been accidents at all, have they? Something's happening here, and if you tell me what it is, maybe I can help.''

Joe sighed. She had a point, but the last thing he needed was to be worrying about Ronnie following them around right now.

"Maybe you can help," Frank said suddenly. "Tell us how Santos got his job with the agency.''

"What?'' Ronnie looked confused.

"How did Santos get a job with your modeling agency?'' Frank repeated. "From what Joe was saying, Thorne doesn't like him, and he doesn't know the first thing about photography.''

"Oh.'' She shook her head. "Is that all you want to know?''

Joe nodded. "That's all.''

She folded her arms across her chest. "If I tell you, I want an explanation tomorrow—for everything.''

"How about the day after?'' Joe said. He felt pretty confident they'd have things wrapped up by then.

"Okay," she said. "It's really very simple. Steven can get whatever job he wants. His father owns the agency."

"Tomorrow," Joe said, pulling their car up to the entrance to the site, "we make sure we get through to Richards and tell him everything."

Frank nodded and climbed out of the car. He moved around to the professor's side to help him out. Frank was kicking himself for the clue he'd missed—the pottery Sara had pointed out to him at the party. She'd even told him the agency's owner had ordered a case full of it recently. He'd be willing to bet that the pieces Sara had sold were the same ones Richards had found the artifacts in.

The only question he had left was whether or not Santos's father was involved in the smuggling, too.

"Are you sure you're all right to do this, Professor?" Joe asked. "We could come with you."

Ortega shook his head. "When I talked to him, Alfredo sounded terrified of the police. Of Hoyil. He'd probably think you two were policemen."

Frank and the professor followed Joe up the dirt road till they came to a small ticket booth by the entrance to the ruins. Off to his right Frank saw the pyramid Acosta had chosen as the rendezvous point. He and Joe planned to wait in the jungle nearby, to keep an eye on the professor. After all, it might be Acosta who was involved with Santos and the other smugglers.

Just then Frank heard the sound of a car approaching. Headlights bobbed through the jungle foliage flanking the entrance to the ruins.

"That could be him." Frank touched the professor lightly on the arm. "We'll be watching."

Ortega nodded, and Frank and Joe disappeared into the jungle.

"Watch out for huge open pits," Frank whispered over his shoulder as he led the way down a trail that circled around the pyramid.

"Very funny," Joe said, slapping at the air. "The biggest danger here is mosquitoes."

As they crouched down in the middle of a thick grove of trees to wait, Frank decided his brother was right. The jungle was alive with the buzzing of a million insects, and it seemed as if every single one of them wanted to bite him. The car they heard had better be Acosta's, he thought, or he was going to get eaten alive.

They sat there for twenty of the most uncomfortable minutes of his life before Frank finally stood up.

"I guess that wasn't Acosta," he said.

"Well, where is he?" Joe asked. "I don't like the idea of the professor standing around all night."

Frank studied Ortega, who was still standing in the clearing at the base of the pyramid, peering about anxiously.

"We'll give him a bit more time," he said, scanning the jungle again. For the first time Frank noticed construction equipment off to the right of the pyramid. A bulldozer, several large sections of pipe—it looked as if they were building some kind of drainage system for the site.

"Professor!"

The sudden cry came from the top of the pyramid.

Frank recognized the voice.

"Alfredo," Ortega said, starting for the pyramid. "What are you doing up there?"

Frank peered up at the man at the top of the pyramid. It was Santos! He must have sneaked through the jungle and come up the other side of the pyramid to surprise Ortega.

"Waiting for you, naturally," the gunman said. He held something down at his side. The rifle?

"Professor!" Frank yelled. "Get out of there! It's a trap!"

Both men turned at the sound of his voice.

Then a third man appeared at the top of the pyramid.

"Vinicio!" Joe said.

Frank had no idea who the man was, but he was huge.

Santos clambered down the last few steps of the pyramid toward the professor. Ortega, frightened by Santos's sudden advance, stepped back and stumbled, falling to the ground.

118

Frank saw that this time Santos wasn't carrying a gun. He had a machete. The blade glinted in the moonlight as Santos raised it over his head.

"Now, Professor," he said, stepping forward, "I'll finish the job."

Chapter
15

JOE WAS ALREADY racing toward Ortega, who
was still lying on the ground.

As Santos started to lower the machete Joe
tackled him from behind. They both pitched forward, Santos crying out in pain as the machete
slipped from his grasp and clattered against the
stones lining the base of the pyramid.

The two of them struggled, rolling over the
cold, hard ground. Joe was easily the stronger
of the two, but the other man was slippery.
Every time Joe thought he had him pinned Santos managed to slip out of his grasp. As they
fought Joe looked out of the corner of his eye
and saw Frank and Vinicio circling each other
warily. The sound of a motorcycle somewhere
in the distance distracted Joe for a moment.

He's going to need help with that guy, Joe told himself. He managed to break free just long enough to deliver a hard right to Santos's jaw. The man fell back, stunned.

Frank tried a side kick, which slammed into the driver's chest, sending him reeling back a couple of steps. Vinicio didn't go down, though, and when Frank came back with another side kick the big man was ready.

Vinicio caught Frank's foot and hung on, spinning him around in the air, finally slamming him against one of the pyramid's stone steps with a sickening crack. Frank lay still on the ground.

"Your turn next, Joe," a voice said from behind them.

Joe spun around to see Lieutenant Hoyil step out of the jungle, a gun in his hand.

He'd been right all along about Hoyil, Joe realized, but how had the lieutenant known to come here?

"Lieutenant!" Santos smiled and stepped away from Frank. "I'm very glad to see you."

"You should be. It's a good thing I decided to keep an eye on you tonight," Hoyil said, frowning. "You could have ruined everything."

"It was an opportunity to have the professor disappear quietly. I didn't know these two would show up."

"We can discuss it later," Hoyil said, clearly in charge.

"What do we do with them now?" Santos asked. "We can't just let them go."

"Of course not," Hoyil said. "But we know the professor and his two young friends are smugglers, don't we?" He smiled. "We should let them look for new artifacts to smuggle."

Joe didn't like the sound of that.

Hoyil marched them at least a mile into the jungle, according to Frank's best estimate, before stopping in front of a small pyramid.

"You recognize this place, of course, Professor," he said.

"Of course," Ortega said. "The lesser pyramid. This is where we found Cloud Ixmix's tomb."

"A magnificent discovery. I come here as often as possible," the lieutenant said. "Let me take this opportunity to congratulate you on it." He pointed toward an entranceway at the base of the pyramid. "Shall we go inside?"

He produced a small flashlight and led the way into a narrow passageway, which ended about fifteen feet inside the pyramid. The right-hand wall of the passageway was made of the same stones as the pyramid outside.

Ten feet inside the entrance the left-hand wall disappeared entirely. A fifteen-foot-square room, totally barren, lay beyond it. Two huge wooden support posts flanked the entrance to the chamber.

"Cloud Ixmix's tomb," Hoyil said, shining his

light inside. He held the gun at his side with his other hand, keeping his finger on the trigger. "Can you imagine what it was like a thousand years ago? Filled with all the jade and gold Ixmix's subjects could gather?"

"Go on," Hoyil said, waving them forward with his gun. "Take a closer look."

Vinicio stood behind Frank. Santos had the machete in his hand again, and Hoyil had a gun. There was nothing else any of them could do.

Frank stepped into the tomb, and Ortega and Joe followed.

"What do you intend to do?" Ortega asked.

Hoyil stepped up to one of the wooden support beams. "They put these in a few weeks ago to shore up the structure, which was starting to collapse. You can see some of the rubble underneath your feet." He motioned Vinicio forward. "A couple of well-placed kicks should bring it down."

He nodded to the driver, who reared back savagely and kicked at the post, which gave a loud crack.

"I'm giving you a chance to make history all over again, Professor," Hoyil said. "Perhaps you will find another hidden tomb. Or who knows? In a thousand years, you and your friends may be the ones being discovered."

A huge stone fell from the ceiling, narrowly missing Vinicio.

"Wait a minute," Joe said. "People are going

to know there's been a cave-in here. They're going to find us."

"And what will they think?" Hoyil asked. "That you were killed by a police lieutenant? Or that a thief returned to the scene of his crimes, and that he and his friends were trapped in a terrible accident?"

Joe couldn't argue with that. He could see the headlines himself.

"Goodbye, Professor. Goodbye, Frank and Joe," Hoyil said. He turned and nodded to Vinicio.

The driver kicked again at the final support beam, which now cracked in half. For a second the roof held, and Hoyil, Santos, and Vinicio made their escape.

Frank jumped backward as the ceiling crashed down in front of him. He tasted a thick cloud of dust in the air and waved it away from in front of his face.

"Joe! Professor! Are you okay?"

"I'm fine, Frank," Ortega called out.

"Joe!" he yelled again. "Where are you?"

Someone coughed in front of him.

"Right here." His brother began coughing violently. Frank followed Joe's coughing until he found him and sat down beside his brother.

"I'm okay," Joe said, catching his breath. "I just caught a faceful of dirt."

"All right, then," Frank said. "Let's see what we can do about getting out of here." He felt his way in the darkness to the pile of rubble that now covered the entrance to the chamber.

It was bad. Some of the stones that blocked their way were too big for him to get his arms around them.

"Professor," he said, "is there any other way out of here?"

"I'm afraid not."

"We're going to have to dig ourselves out, then," Frank said, kneeling down in front of the cave-in. He dug into the rubble, grabbing hold of a cinder-block–size piece of rubble. As he pulled at it he felt the stone crumble in his hands.

This was going to take forever.

"Hold on," Joe said. Frank felt his brother brush past and sit down on the other side of him. "It'll go faster if we work at the same spot."

He nodded, and they began digging.

"How long do you think we have before the air runs out in here?" Joe asked.

"Not long," he said. In fact, it was getting hard to breathe already.

Frank reached forward again with his right hand and grabbed hold of a good-size rock. He yanked hard at it, but it wouldn't budge.

Then, behind him, Frank heard something move.

"Professor? Was that you?"

"No," Ortega called back weakly. "I have no idea what that was."

Frank heard it again, closer this time. It sounded like something was coming toward them through the walls of the pyramid. Some kind of animal, maybe?

"Frank," Joe said, "that's you, right? Don't play games anymore."

"It's not me, Joe," he said quietly.

There was the sound of something hard hitting against the wall of rubble before them, and then dirt and debris striking the chamber floor.

"Whatever it is," Frank said, "it's in the cave with us now."

"Great," Joe said. "Just when I was getting used to the idea of suffocating to death."

Ignoring his brother, Frank began feeling around the site of the cave-in with his hands. It sounded as if the noise had come from the front of the chamber.

Suddenly he touched something hard, cold, and slick with dirt. A second later he realized what it was.

"What's going on?" Ortega asked.

"It's a pipe," he said. Now he could feel the gentle pressure of air coming through it from the other side. "Someone must be on the other side of the passageway trying to rescue us!"

"But who?" Joe asked.

"Hey! Are you guys okay in there?"

For a second Frank thought he'd imagined the voice, it was so faint and muffled. Then he realized where it was coming from.

He put his ear up to the end of the pipe and listened again.

This time he heard their rescuer loud and clear. He even recognized her voice.

"Hey, Joe," he said, standing up and backing away from the pipe. "Come here and talk to your dinner date."

"That's one you owe me now," Ronnie said.

Joe nodded and held his head out the car window for a minute, trying to let the wind blow away the dirt that still coated his hair. He'd caught a glimpse of himself in the rearview mirror. Frank didn't look much better.

Professor Ortega looked a lot worse. The older man had fallen asleep leaning up against the passenger-side window in the front seat, next to Frank. Joe was afraid his wound was going to start bleeding again.

Joe turned to Ronnie, who sat next to him in the backseat, and smiled. "I don't know what made you decide to do it, but I'm glad you followed us."

"Well, I didn't mean to," she said. "At least not at first. I rode around on Thome's motorcycle for a while, but the more I thought about what you'd said, the angrier I got. I was going to come back and—"

"Yell at me?"

"Talk to you. Don't interrupt. But when I arrived you were just pulling out of the motel. So I decided to see where you were going.''

Joe nodded. He knew the rest: Ronnie had heard the cave-in and seen Santos and his companions emerge from the pyramid without them. She'd ridden immediately to the nearest village and roused a half dozen men to help dig them out.

Ortega suddenly shifted in the front seat and cried out in his sleep.

Joe leaned over the seat to look at the professor again and frowned.

"How far are we from Cancún?" Joe asked. Their plan was to return there and dump the entire case into Montoya's lap. He and Frank had agreed it was too dangerous to be working on their own now.

Frank turned on the light above the rearview mirror and glanced at the map next to him on the front seat. "The next left is the coast highway. From there Cancún's about an hour.''

The sun was just coming up; that meant they'd be there by early morning.

He frowned. "I don't know, Frank. I think we should stop somewhere sooner so we can check the professor's shoulder. He doesn't look good to me."

"Why not take him to the mansion?" Ronnie asked. "Steven gave all of us keys. It's only about fifteen minutes from here."

"Sounds good to me," Joe said.

"All right." Frank nodded. "The mansion it is, then."

It took them almost twenty minutes to reach the house, but after Frank had a chance to look at the professor's wound he was glad Joe had suggested that they stop.

"The stitches were starting to tear a little, Professor," Frank said. He finished dressing Ortega's wound with some gauze Ronnie had found. "The wound could have torn open, and you'd have started bleeding again."

"Are we all set, then?" Joe asked. He'd barely moved from the front doorway for the past fifteen minutes.

"What's the rush?" Ronnie asked. She'd taken the time to change into new jeans and a sweatshirt and pin her hair up. "We could get something to eat. There's plenty of food left over from the party."

Frank shook his head. "It's time to let the authorities know what's going on."

Joe nodded. "Let's go, Ronnie. We can eat in Cancún. I know this great restaurant."

As Frank turned to reach for the front doorknob, the door swung open on its own.

A man Joe had never seen before walked through.

"Mr. Conrado!" Ronnie said. "What are you doing here?"

Chapter

16

CONRADO! For a minute Joe didn't understand. Conrado was the guy who'd given the benefit back in Bayport, the guy whose wife had been wearing the jade piece that had started this whole thing—

Suddenly the pieces fell into place for Frank, too. He felt as if he'd been punched in the stomach.

"I should be asking you and your friends that question, Ronnie," he said. "After all, I own this house."

He waved his hand, and Hoyil and Santos stepped through the door behind him, guns drawn.

"But then, my associates have been telling me what's happening." He smiled. "It's a good thing I decided to fly down this morning," Conrado said. "Otherwise we all might have missed one another." He turned to Frank. "How pleasant to see you again."

"Again?" Ronnie shook her head. "You know him?"

"Unfortunately," Frank said.

"Come, Frank. We're old friends. And this other young man must be your brother. Joe, isn't it?"

"Wait," Ronnie said. "What's going on?"

Joe shook his head glumly. "You're looking at the brains behind the entire smuggling operation."

"Mr. Conrado?" Ronnie said. "But he's just—he owns the mansion and the modeling agency."

"And an awful lot," Frank said, "of Mayan artifacts."

"It's amazing," Conrado said, "how much trouble one unexpected guest can be."

It took Frank a minute, but he finally understood what Conrado was talking about.

"Clint. He wasn't supposed to be at your party."

Conrado nodded. "If he hadn't shown up and recognized that jade piece—"

"Your little frame-up of the professor would have worked just fine," Joe said.

"Luz would never have believed you!" Ortega exclaimed, sitting up on the couch and gesturing angrily. Frank could see the strain on his face. "She would have found out the truth!"

"A minor customs official?" Hoyil said. "Never. No one would have listened to her."

Santos smiled. "And if she made too much noise, we could have always arranged an accident of some sort."

"I don't think that would have worked," Joe said. "You're not too good at that kind of thing."

"Quiet!" Santos said angrily, stepping forward.

"Enough, Steven," Conrado said. He shook his head. "An impetuous young man, my son. Takes after his mother's side of the family. My first wife, that is. It's her last name that he uses professionally."

"Look, no one's been killed," Frank said. "Let us all go now, and things won't be so bad for you."

"Voluntarily send myself to jail? I have no doubt I could arrange a comfortable term of imprisonment here, but"—he shook his head— "American justice is not quite that easy to buy. No, I'm afraid we are going to have to finish what we have started."

He smiled. "If you would all follow me, please."

With Hoyil bringing up the rear, Conrado led them single file out the back of the mansion and down to the boat house Joe had seen the night of the party. Santos walked directly behind Joe, digging his gun into Joe's back.

Inside the boat house they found a huge cabin cruiser, easily sixty feet long.

"It's a lovely day for a cruise, don't you think?" he asked, stepping from the dock onto the boat. He motioned for them all to follow. "I'm sure no one could blame you, Ronnie—least of all the owner—for 'borrowing' his boat."

Joe understood instantly.

"You're going to blow us up at sea."

Conrado nodded his head. "I am very impressed. You're as smart as your brother." His voice hardened. "Steven, you and the lieutenant take them below. Put them in the main cabin."

Santos and Hoyil marched the four of them down through the ship's galley and through the interior of the ship. The main cabin turned out to occupy almost the entire forward part of the boat, Frank observed. The room had two double-decker bunks that came together in a V at the bow, and several large pieces of mahogany furniture. Under different circumstances Frank would have enjoyed spending time here.

"I'm afraid this time it really is goodbye," Hoyil said. The lieutenant stood at the door of the cabin and smiled. "I wanted to thank you for returning to the house to meet us, by the way."

He pulled the door shut and locked it behind him.

Ortega sat down heavily on one of the bottom bunks. Joe bent down and looked at the professor's bandage. He hadn't had a chance to wrap it as tightly as he would have liked.

"I'm all right," Ortega said, waving him off. "You worry about getting us out of here."

"That's not going to be easy," Frank said. There were two small portholes on either side of the cabin, and he didn't think they'd be able to squeeze through those.

He heard the motor start up and felt the boat begin to move away from the dock. "I figure we have about five minutes till we get far enough out to sea," he said.

"That doesn't leave us a whole lot of time," Joe commented. "Hey, Professor? Any Mayan gods of the ocean we can pray to?"

Ortega shook his head. "I think this time we're on our own."

"That's all right," Joe said suddenly. His eyes came to rest on Ronnie. More specifically, on her hair. "I've got an idea."

Ronnie frowned. "Why are you staring at me?"

"Don't take this the wrong way," he said, "but would you let down your hair?"

It took about a minute to bend the pins that had been holding Ronnie's hair up into a makeshift lock pick, and another minute to open the door to their cabin.

"All right," Joe said. "Professor, Ronnie—"

"Don't you dare tell me to stay here," Ronnie said, glaring at him.

Joe glared right back. "Don't interrupt me."

"Come on, you two," Frank said. Joe could swear his brother was smiling as he stepped past Joe and out into the corridor. "You both follow me. Professor, stay here."

Joe stepped out behind him. Just ahead he could see the ship's galley and steps leading up to the main deck. There was no one in sight.

"They might have left already, Frank."

His brother shook his head. "I don't think so."

Suddenly a trapdoor in the middle of the galley floor flew open, and Lieutenant Hoyil climbed out.

There was no place for them to go! If the lieutenant turned around, they were caught.

Hoyil didn't even pause, though. He quickly passed through the galley and ran up onto the main deck.

"The engine room," Frank whispered pointing to the open hatchway. "I'll bet he just planted the bomb down there."

"Go for it," Joe said as his brother stepped forward and disappeared silently down the trapdoor.

Joe turned to Ronnie. "Wait here," he said. "Don't worry. I'll be right back."

She opened her mouth for a second, then nodded. "All right."

Keeping low, Joe climbed the short flight of stairs out of the galley and into the dining area, right next to the main deck. At the stern of the boat Conrado and Santos were lowering the dinghy into the ocean. Almost at the same instant he heard someone pacing above. Hoyil, he thought. He must be locking down the wheel so the boat won't drift off course.

Joe backed down the stairs and waved Ronnie forward.

"They're getting ready to abandon ship," he whispered. "I'm going to try to lure them away from the dingy. Stay out of sight until they start chasing me, then take their boat and get to shore. Bring help."

"But—" Ronnie began.

"No time for anything else," he said.

"All right," she said. "Be careful."

"You, too." Joe climbed out onto the main deck and started up the stairs that led to the captain's cockpit. His plan was to surprise Hoyil and get control of the boat. Conrado and Santos would have to come after him then.

But halfway up the stairs Hoyil turned and saw him.

"Conrado!" the lieutenant cried instantly, drawing his gun. "They're free!"

So much for surprises.

Joe spun and leapt down the flight of stairs in a single bound, landing hard on the main deck. He spun again, heading for the bow. A quick glance behind told him his plan was at least partially working: Santos had moved away from the dinghy and was hot on his heels.

As he raced down the narrow gangway leading to the front deck someone fired a shot. It ricocheted off the railing next to him.

He leapt forward, hitting the front deck with his shoulder and rolling to his feet again.

Hoyil came down the gangway on one side of the boat. A split second later Santos came around on the other side.

Joe spun around, desperately looking for a way out. For a minute he even thought about jumping overboard.

"Don't try it, Hardy," Santos said, advancing toward him. "You'll be dead before you hit the water."

Chapter
17

AS FRANK CLIMBED DOWN into the dimly lit engine room the smell of gasoline rose up to meet him.

Hoyil must have doused it with every spare drop of fuel on board, he thought. Conrado was leaving nothing to chance.

As his eyes adjusted to the darkness Frank quickly picked out the explosive the lieutenant had planted. It was a single stick of dynamite sitting right on top of the boat's engine. He walked over and picked up the bomb, breathing a sigh of relief as he examined it.

There was a simple timing device attached to the dynamite. Two thin wires, a small battery, and a digital clock with bright red numerals that told him he had about three hundred seconds—

five minutes—before it went off. This was the easiest kind of bomb to disarm; he'd done it a dozen times before without a hitch. All he had to do was disconnect the ground wire from the dynamite.

Except it was too dark to see which wire was the ground.

The clock now read two hundred and eighty seconds.

Frank walked the bomb over to the ladder leading into the galley. There should be enough light there to see which wire was which, he thought.

But the leads were unmarked. Two hundred forty seconds.

If he guessed wrong and pulled the positive lead, the bomb would blow up in his face. He could simply take out the battery, but even doing that might send enough current through the circuit to trigger the device.

Two hundred seconds.

He was going to have to throw the bomb overboard. He started up the ladder, cradling it against his chest, when he heard shots ring out above, and he froze.

The clock read one hundred eighty seconds.

Three minutes.

"Where's your brother?" Santos asked, waving his gun.

"I don't know." Joe put his hands up slowly.

"Check below, Steven," Hoyil said, stepping forward. "I'll keep an eye on this one."

Joe's eyes strayed to the lieutenant for a second, then widened involuntarily.

Ronnie was right behind him, a small fire extinguisher held high above her head. She swung it hard, and Hoyil crumpled.

Santos turned reflexively at the noise. That gave Joe his chance.

He sprang forward, tackling him at the waist, slamming the man back into the narrow wooden railing that circled the main deck.

Joe heard a sudden crack, and suddenly he lost control. The two of them were plunging overboard into the ocean!

He hit the water face first. The impact stunned him, and he lost his grip on Santos. For a second he flailed about in the ocean.

"Joe! Look out!"

It was Ronnie. He turned just in time to see Santos pointing his gun directly at him.

He lunged forward and caught the man's wrist. The gun shot out of Santos's grasp and disappeared beneath the waves.

With a cry Santos swung at him with his other arm. But it was a halfhearted effort in the water, almost in slow motion. Joe grabbed the arm and yanked him forward, grabbing him in a headlock.

Just then he heard the sound of an approaching outboard motor. He turned and saw Conrado bearing down on them in the dinghy!

"Let him go!" Conrado yelled, raising a gun of his own. He took aim and fired.

Joe realized that it didn't matter if he let go or not.

Conrado was going to kill him, anyway.

The clock read sixty seconds. Frank couldn't wait any longer.

Gunfight or not—he had to get rid of the bomb.

He stepped up and out of the engine room and almost ran smack into Professor Ortega.

"Frank!" The man's eyes widened as he caught sight of the bomb. "What's going on?"

"I'm getting rid of this, Professor. Other than that, I don't know."

Ortega followed him out onto the main deck. There was no one in sight.

"Joe? Ronnie?" he called out.

"Frank! Up here!"

He ran around to the front of the boat, where he found Ronnie holding a gun on Hoyil. The lieutenant was sitting up on the deck, rubbing the back of his head.

"Frank!"

"Where's Joe?" he asked.

"I don't know," she said. "He and Steven fell overboard, and then Conrado shot at him. Steven and Conrado are getting away!"

She pointed out over the bow of the boat,

where Frank could see a small dinghy disappearing in the distance.

"First things first," Frank said, glancing down at the bomb. Thirty seconds. "I've got to get rid of this. Everybody get behind me." He looked over the starboard side of the boat. There was nothing in sight for miles.

"Ready?" He cocked his arm back as if he were going to pass a football.

"Hold it!"

Frank stopped in his tracks. "Joe!"

His brother was treading water out in the ocean, about fifty yards in front of him.

"You're alive!" Ronnie yelled.

"So far," Joe called back. "As long as Frank throws that off the other side of the boat!"

"No problem," his brother said. Ten seconds.

He ran to the stern of the boat and threw the bomb as far out over the ocean as he could.

The bomb exploded in midair. Frank swallowed.

The timer had been off by more than a few seconds.

Joe swam quickly back to the cruiser, where Frank helped pull him aboard.

"You okay?"

Joe nodded, catching his breath. "I'm fine, but Conrado and Steven are getting away."

Just then Hoyil came marching around to them, Ronnie a step behind him, holding his gun. Ortega followed her.

"Joe," she said. "You're all right!"

"So far," he said. "I'd be a lot better if we could get hold of Conrado and Santos."

"You'll never catch them," Hoyil sneered.

"You shut up," Ronnie said, leveling the gun at him.

Joe smiled at her. "Come on. Let's get after those two."

They all climbed up to the top deck, where Frank took the wheel. He gunned the engine, quickly closing the gap between them and the dinghy. Then he realized Conrado wasn't heading back to his mansion.

"He's making for that beach up there." Frank pointed up ahead, slowing the boat down. "It'll be too shallow for us to follow in this thing."

"We can swim it," Joe said. "It can't be more than a mile." He turned back to Ronnie.

"Think you can get this back to the boat house?"

She hesitated. "I've never driven a boat before."

"Think of it as a racing car," Joe said.

"Oh." She smiled. "In that case, no problem." She handed the gun to Ortega, who kept it leveled at Hoyil.

"While you're at it, see if you can raise the police on that." Frank pointed to the shortwave radio next to the instrument panel. "In fact, see if you can get hold of Luz Montoya."

"Who?"

"I'll fill her in," Ortega said. "Now, hurry, you two. They're getting away."

Frank stepped back from the wheel. "It's all yours, Ronnie. Come on, Joe." He turned and bounded down the stairs a few steps ahead of his brother.

"Be careful!" Ronnie shouted after them.

Frank dived into the ocean and began swimming with long, powerful strokes. He reached shore a couple of hundred yards ahead of Joe, and he found the dinghy, deserted. Farther up the beach he saw a refreshment stand and some changing rooms.

Joe came ashore and jogged up next to him. "Any sign of them?"

Frank shook his head, pointing toward the refreshment stand. "I say we try up there."

They were about halfway to the stand when people suddenly started swarming onto the beach, yelling.

The two broke into a run. As they drew closer Joe saw the refreshment stand was just the back half of a much larger restaurant from which the people—most of whom looked like American tourists—were pouring. He and Frank fought their way past the crowd just in time to see a red sedan speed out of the restaurant's parking lot.

Santos was at the wheel, with Conrado in the seat next to him.

"They're getting away!"

"And we don't have anything to follow in," Joe said. He scanned the parking lot frantically. "There. See that?" He grabbed Frank by the shoulder and spun him around so he could see the tour bus parked at the side of the restaurant.

"The bus?" Frank asked. "What can you do with that?"

Joe ran to the driver's side window, which was partially open, reached inside, and found the door release lever.

"Borrow it for a little while," Joe said, smiling as the door hissed open. Sure enough, the keys were in the ignition. "Those tourists look like they'll want to relax a bit before getting back on the road, anyway."

"He was heading north on the coast highway," Frank said as Joe backed the bus out of the parking lot. "Probably to Cancún."

"It's a big place," Joe said. "We're going to need a lot of help finding them if we don't catch up to him on the road."

"We'll get help," Frank said. "Montoya and Richards can vouch for us with the authorities. There's nowhere Conrado can go."

His brother was right. Conrado was through. If he were in the man's shoes, he wouldn't head back to Cancún. He wouldn't even stay in Mexico.

In fact, there was really only one place he would go.

"Frank. Conrado said he flew in himself this morning."

"Right," his brother said. "So?"

Joe waited for him to get it.

"He's got a private plane!" Frank said suddenly. "That's it. He's on his way to the airport."

"And so are we," Joe said.

Ten minutes later he pulled the bus up in front of the local aviation terminal. He and Frank dashed into the building.

"We're looking for a man called Jorge Conrado," Frank said to the man behind the information counter. "He has a private plane here—"

"Mr. Conrado," the clerk said. "I don't even need to check the computer for that. You just missed him. He and his son are in that little two-seater out there. The small black one." The man pointed to the window behind him, where the airport runways were visible.

Frank saw Conrado's aircraft just moving out onto the runway, two other planes ahead of it.

"Let's go!" Joe said, bursting through a door marked Local Aviation Only.

"Wait a minute!" the man called after them. "You can't go through there!"

Ignoring him, Frank followed Joe out the door and into a huge aircraft hangar filled with dozens of smaller planes. The hangar door was open.

Out on the runway, Conrado's plane was next in line to take off.

"We've got to stop him!" Joe said.

"How are we going to do that? Grab onto the wings and slow him down?"

Just then a fully loaded luggage cart drove by the front of the hangar. Frank thought the man behind the wheel looked familiar.

"And I used to care about the kind of car I drove," Joe said, breaking into a run. "Come on, Frank. This isn't over yet."

When they were about twenty feet away the driver saw Joe coming. He immediately stopped the cart and jumped out.

The man charged Joe. At the last possible second Joe spun and dodged.

"Sorry, Ed," Joe called over his shoulder as he jumped into the cart. Frank hopped in beside him.

"Isn't that the same guy who—"

"Later," Joe said, stepping on the gas. He headed directly across the airfield until the cart was right in the middle of the runway. Then he turned so it was facing straight at Conrado's plane.

"I hope you know what you're doing," Frank said.

"I'm not sure," Joe said, smiling tightly. He accelerated. "I've never played chicken with a luggage cart before."

Conrado was beginning his takeoff run, heading straight for them.

"I don't think he's going to stop," Frank said, watching the plane gather speed.

"Well, guess what." Joe pressed his foot to the floor even harder.

"Neither are we."

Chapter

18

THE PLANE drew closer and closer. Through the cockpit glass Joe could see both Santos and Conrado.

They were going to crash any second!

"Jump when I say go," he said. "Ready—"

Joe was close enough to see the expression on Conrado's face as his son suddenly grabbed the wheel from him and twisted it.

The plane lurched violently to one side, one wheel scraping against the driver's side of the luggage cart, slamming into Frank. Both of them tumbled out of the cart and onto the runway, landing in the middle of a huge pile of luggage.

Joe sat up slowly, still stunned from the impact, and watched Conrado's plane veer off wildly across the runway, completely out of control!

Sirens began to wail. Joe watched a squad of emergency vehicles from the main terminal building come tearing down the runway, lights flashing.

Conrado's plane had rolled to a stop at the edge of the airfield, the left tire on the landing gear completely flat. Santos stepped out of the plane onto the wing and then jumped to the ground, running for the safety of the jungle.

"I'll get him," Joe said to Frank. He tackled the man from behind before he'd gotten more than twenty yards.

"Some people," he said, shaking his head at Santos, "just never learn."

The first ambulance reached the aircraft at the same time Frank did. He shrugged away their offers of assistance, cupped his hands together, and called up to the plane.

'Come on out, Conrado! It's all over."

A few seconds later the man emerged, bleeding from a large cut over one eye. For once he wasn't smiling.

"You're going to jail," Frank said, taking his arm. "For a long time."

"We'll see about that." Conrado shrugged. "I have a lot of friends in this country."

No doubt many judges among them, Frank thought as he brought the man over to where Joe was holding Santos.

Two police cars came cruising down the runway toward them. As the first drew up, Hunt Richards stepped out of the back seat.

"Agent Richards!" Frank said. "What are you doing here?"

"I've been here for days, kid," Richards said, smiling. "You didn't think I was really going to leave you alone with Ortega, did you?" He frowned. "Where is the professor, by the way?"

"Never mind him," Frank said, dragging Conrado forward. "Here's your smuggler."

"Jorge Conrado," Richards said. "Pleased to meet you." He turned to Frank and explained. "I was with the local police when the Coast Guard report came in."

Ronnie must have gotten the message through, then. Good, thought Frank. He went over the events of the last few days for Richards. "And I'd take a look at some of the other pieces in his house back in America if I were you," he finished. "I'd be surprised if this was the first smuggling ring he's been involved with."

"Wait a minute!" Conrado said, eyes pleading. "You can't let him take me back to America!"

"You're an American citizen," Richards said. "I don't think the authorities will have any problem sending you back with me to stand trial. And as for your son"—he motioned to a couple of police officers who took hold of both Conrado and Santos—"I'm sure he'll want to stay with his loving father."

"So long, you two," he said, shaking hands

with first Frank, then Joe. "See if you can stay out of trouble for the rest of your trip."

As Richards drove off another police car pulled up. The professor and Ronnie climbed out of this one.

"Don't tell me," Ronnie said, frowning as she caught sight of the wrecked airplane at the edge of the roadway. "I've missed all the excitement again."

"We could take you back to Cobá," Joe suggested. "I'll bet there's some excitement going on there right about now. At the modeling shoot?"

"Oh, my gosh! I forgot all about that. Thome's going to kill me!"

"Well, I think you should consider a career change, anyway," Joe said. "You're a much better detective than a model."

Ronnie frowned. "Thanks," she said. "I think."

"Professor," Frank said, "shouldn't you be resting somewhere?" Ortega still looked exhausted, though not so much as earlier.

"He should be back in the hospital," Joe said firmly. "Where somebody can take a look at his wound."

Ortega touched his shoulder and winced. "All right. But before I go back to that hospital food," he said, "one meal. Please. I've been in Mexico for three days and haven't tasted a taco yet."

"I know just the place," Frank said, smiling.

"No." Ortega held up his hand. "I insist. I know where to go. There's a little restaurant just outside the hotel called Harry's. You'll love it."

Frank winked at Joe as he and the professor walked off in the direction of the main terminal.

"And you?" Ronnie asked, turning to Joe. "What are your plans for the rest of your trip?"

"Well," Joe said, "I, er, have to return a bus."

"A bus?" She raised an eyebrow.

"A bus." Joe nodded. "Want to come with me?"

Ronnie thought a moment, then smiled. "Sure, but only if I can drive."

He took her arm and started down the runway.

"El americano loco! El americano loco!"

Joe turned and saw Eduardo running toward him.

"Come on," he said, taking Ronnie's arm. "I'll race you back to the parking lot."

Frank and Joe's next case:

A cool million in cash can raise temperatures in even the hottest towns, and no city on earth sizzles like Las Vegas, Nevada. The Hardys have come to the Camelot Casino so Frank can compete in the National Computer Chess Championship. But before the first move is made, the boys find themselves pawns in a chilling kidnapping caper.

The daughter of a ruthless local businessman is the victim, and Frank and Joe are prime suspects. The only way to clear their name is find the girl and grab her abductors. But the kidnappers are masters of the game. The Hardys must watch their step and make every move count—or they may end up walking into a deadly desert trap . . . in *Final Gambit,* Case #62 in The Hardy Boys Casefiles™.